T

Awesome

Adventures of

Poppy and Amelia

Maddy Harrisis lives in Bristol with her mum and dad and her little brother Ollie. She likes drawing, climbing trees, and spending time with her friends.

Misha Herwin is a writer of books for children and adults, including *The Adventures of Letty Parker*, a series for 8-12 year olds. She lives in Staffordshire in a house with a dragon in the garden, and is Maddy's granny.

The Awesome Adventures of Poppy and Amelia

Maddy Harrisis
and
Misha Herwin

The Penkhull Press

Published by the Penkhull Press
www.penkhullpress.co.uk

Acknowledgements

Maddy and Misha would like to thank everyone who helped make this book. *The Awesome Adventures of Poppy and Amelia* has been great fun to write but we couldn't have done it without Jan Edwards and her editing skills; the Renegade Writers who listened as the story unfolded every Wednesday and gave brilliant feedback; Grandpa Mike and his proofreading; and Peter Coleborn who designed the book and the absolutely awesome cover.

Thank you everyone!

**For Ollie,
the best little brother in the world**

Preface

When I started doing some home-schooling via Skype with Maddy during lockdown I had no idea that we would end up writing a book together. *The Awesome Adventures of Poppy and Amelia* began with a story told at the end of each lesson and quickly grew into a series of adventures as the apprentice witches learned more about their craft.

Once we had the stories then came the writing and editing. It took some time but we've enjoyed the whole process and finally getting everything together has been more than exciting.

We hope you will have as much fun reading about Poppy, Amelia and Mia as we did writing about them.

To spread the joy, we've decided that profits from the book will go to Leukaemia Research, in memory of Posy Miller, my daughter and Maddy's aunt.

—Misha

Chapter 1

POPPY RACED DOWN the corridor. She was late for history and class 7C were already in the classroom, laughing, chatting, sending texts, and making loud burping noises while Mr Harrison, the supply teacher, was trying to take the register. As Poppy was halfway through the door he turned and glared at her.

Clicking his fingers, he pointed and said, "Poppy Barrington, get out and don't let me see you for the rest of the day."

"That's not fair, sir. Poppy hasn't done anything," Amelia, her best friend, protested.

"If you're going to question my decisions, you can go too."

As Amelia stood up the rest of the class shouted and booed.

"Silence, you horrible little toads." Mr Harrison clicked his fingers once again, and in a single moment he was the only person in the room. There was not one pupil to be seen – in their place were twenty-eight large, brown wrinkled toads.

"That's more like it," Mr Harrison said.

The toad that was Amelia gave a terrified croak and hopped into the corridor to sit near Poppy's foot. "It's okay, I'll look after you." Poppy stretched out her hand to pick up the toad. The toad turned its head in her direction, but it didn't move. "Oh no!" Poppy gasped. She couldn't see her fingers, or her hands, or any other part of her. "I'm invisible. Mr Harrison must have done it when he pointed at me."

In the classroom the toads were stretching their limbs. Their skins were growing smoother, their bodies longer and thinner and soon 7C were back to normal, except that no one was talking or making a noise.

"That's all right then. The magic doesn't last very long." Poppy checked her hands but she still couldn't see herself. "He's forgotten us, Amelia, but don't worry. I'll remind him." Poppy opened the door a crack. "Please sir," she began.

"Who said that?" Mr Harrison glared at the class. "Didn't I say you were to sit in silence for the rest of the lesson?"

"It's me … Poppy. And I'm still invisible and Amelia is—"

"Silence." He slid his finger across his lips. Poppy retreated as fast as she could, but she was not quick enough. Mr Harrison had taken away her voice and when she tried to speak not a sound came out of her mouth.

Out in the corridor Poppy put her backpack on the ground, unzipped it, and very gently pushed Amelia towards it until she disappeared inside.

Then they waited for the end of the lesson when Poppy was sure Mr Harrison would remove the spell before they could go home, but after the bell rang 7C piled out of the room and he walked straight past without a word.

You can't leave us like this, Poppy thought and chased after him, because if she didn't reach him before he left school they might never be changed back. Amelia would remain a toad and she would be invisible forever. Since neither of them could speak their parents would think they'd gone missing, and nobody would ever know what had really happened.

Poppy ran to the teachers' carpark. She had one last chance to put everything right but when she reached it Mr Harrison was driving out of the gates.

Poppy grabbed her bike from the bike shed and took the shortcut out to the road. She was just in time to see his little yellow car disappearing around the corner and into High Street. Pedalling furiously, she raced down the street, swerving in and out of the traffic. Thrown from side to side in the backpack, Amelia croaked loudly. People on the pavement stopped and pointed. Drivers sounded their horns and stared in disbelief as the bike with its invisible rider tore past. Only Mr Harrison kept looking straight ahead.

At the end of High Street he turned left. Poppy skidded around the bend and followed the car's tail lights until, very suddenly and unexpectedly, they disappeared. She couldn't see where they had gone because the houses in Laburnum Avenue were hidden behind thick hedges and tall trees.

Poppy wasn't going to give up. If she had to, she would search every house in the road. Jumping off her bike, she started back the way she'd come and saw a pair of black iron gates she hadn't noticed before. They were open and beyond them was the yellow car. It was parked in front of a rambling cottage that had a steep roof, windows like startled eyes, and a veranda that ran all the way round to the back.

Propping her bike against the hedge, Poppy ran up the steps to the front door and knocked.

There was a long, long pause, then very, very slowly the door began to open.

Chapter 2

"GOOD EVENING, POPPY," said a tall grey-haired woman in a flowery skirt and dragon earrings. A large ginger cat stood at her side.

"You can see me! And hear me!" Poppy cried in surprise. She lifted her hand to her face then dropped it again as she realised she was still invisible.

"Of course I can. Come in, my dear. We've been waiting for you."

From inside the bag, Amelia gave a warning croak and Poppy remembered that she should never, ever, under any circumstances whatsoever, go into a stranger's house. But what else was she to do? This was an emergency.

She followed the woman down a dusty corridor, through a kitchen and into the back room. The walls were lined with shelves, which were stacked with bottles filled with different coloured liquids; herbs hung from hooks in the ceiling; a fire burned in a black stove; and Mr Harrison sat at an old wooden table, resting his head in his hands.

"Mother, why did you have to let them in?" he groaned.

"Because we can't have them wandering about like that, Morfin. Someone is sure to miss them."

"Do you mean I have to turn them back?"

"It's what you should have done before you left school," Mrs Harrison snapped.

"I know but I wanted to get out of there as fast as I could."

"And now we have a problem."

"We won't tell anyone. I promise." Poppy was afraid that the Harrisons might make them disappear for ever. "Please, take the spell off."

Mrs Harrison glowered at her son. "You conjured the spell. You must remove it."

"Oh!" Mr Harrison groaned and thumped the table. "Why do I have to do this stuff? I hate magic. I never wanted it. Here, take it." He stared at Poppy and raised his hand towards her.

"Stop!" Mrs Harrison said, but it was too late. A flash of emerald light zigzagged across the room and the marmalade cat dived under the table. The green lightning bolt hit Poppy right in the chest, went straight through her, and swished into the backpack so hard that it fell straight off her back.

The air shivered. The room whirled. And then Amelia, with one foot still in the bag, was standing beside Poppy.

"I'm me again!"

"So am I." Poppy waved her hands in delight.

A streak of scarlet whizzed past Mrs Harrison's

right ear. She turned on her son. "Morfin, you've always been hopeless with magic and now you've totally lost control."

Silver sparks shot around the room. The marmalade cat yowled and Mr Harrison looked frightened. "What am I going to do?" he asked.

"You can let us go home," Poppy said hopefully.

"Who asked you?" Mrs Harrison said.

"Sorry." Amelia's lip quivered.

"You've caused nothing but trouble since you came."

"It wasn't our fault," Poppy said. "We didn't ask to be turned into toads or be made invisible."

"If you'd behaved none of this would have happened," Mr Harrison said.

"If you were a proper teacher it wouldn't have either," Amelia said.

"You're right." Mr Harrison slumped across the table again. "I'm useless. I can't do anything right." He looked so miserable that, in spite of the danger they were in, Poppy couldn't help feeling sorry for him.

Shards of indigo splintered against the window and a spider plopped onto the sill. Mrs Harrison swept it onto the floor. "If you girls don't want the magic then say so. Be quick or all Morfin's powers will be yours."

Poppy looked at Amelia. Amelia looked at Poppy. They both nodded.

"Then catch it. Now."

The girls raised their hands and the magic flew into them. Poppy's arms and legs tingled, her hair sparked, her insides fizzed, and her glasses slid down her nose. Amelia's hair stood on end, her body shook and her eyes opened and shut.

"Done." Mrs Harrison clicked her fingers. "Sit down. It will take a few minutes to get over the transference and then you'll feel fine."

"Does this mean we can do magic?" Amelia asked once the shaking and the whirling and the sparking had stopped.

"It means that you have started on a long journey of learning. It won't be easy, but nothing worthwhile ever is." Mrs Harrison glanced at her son. "And you will have to obey the rules."

"Witches have rules?" Poppy said.

"Naturally."

"What are they?"

"That all depends on what sort of witch you are. We are good witches, who care for the earth and everything that is on it. We look after each other and if things go wrong—" Mr Harrison winced "—we put them right."

"What about evil witches, like in stories?" Amelia asked fearfully.

"They care only for themselves. It's best to have nothing to do with them. But enough of that. To start your apprenticeship you will need one of these." Mrs Harrison went over to the dresser and took a book out of a drawer.

"There's only one—" Poppy began then stopped as the witch clicked her fingers and another copy appeared.

"Off you go and don't trouble me again." Mrs Harrison gave them such a fierce look that Poppy's mouth went dry.

"What if there's an emergency?" Amelia said.

"In that case I suppose you will have to, but in general I expect you to read the book and work things out for yourselves. You're not stupid or you wouldn't have found your way here. Marmaduke, show them out."

The marmalade cat emerged from under the table and wound himself around their legs pushing them towards the door, which opened, then slammed shut as soon as they were outside.

"Wow!" Amelia said.

"Whew!" Poppy let out her breath. "Am I glad to be out of there."

"Do you think we really are witches?"

"We must be. We've got this." Poppy held up her book.

The Witches' Handbook. Potions, Spells and Magicks for the Apprentice Witch, it said in spidery, silvery letters. "Apprentice witches, Amelia. That's us."

"Awesome!" Amelia breathed.

"Absolutely awe … some!" Poppy agreed.

They stared at each other, hardly daring to

believe what had happened, then Poppy jumped on her bike and with Amelia clinging on behind rode as fast as she could down Laburnum Avenue and away from the witch's house.

Chapter 3

"YOU'RE LATE BACK from school," Mum said when Poppy finally reached home. "I was beginning to get worried. Next time, text me."

Poppy promised she would and ran upstairs to her bedroom before Mum could ask any awkward questions about what she'd been doing. Shutting the door to keep her little brother Jake out, she sat down on her bed, unzipped her backpack, and took out the *The Witches' Handbook.*

The book smelled old. The pages were thick with crinkly edges and the writing was black and spiky. Poppy leaned closer, worried that she wouldn't be able to read it, when a voice said, "It is usual to start at the beginning. Unless you are searching for a particular spell in which case ask and you will be directed to the correct page."

"What?" Poppy jerked back and the book slid from her lap.

"Be careful," it said, "I am unique. As the property of Poppy Barrington alone, only you can read from my pages. Nevertheless, I wish to be treated with the respect I deserve."

"Sorry." Poppy picked up the book and propped it against her pillow.

"That's better. Less chance of accidents. What is it you want to know?"

"Everything."

"Tea's ready." Mum's voice floated up from the kitchen. "And remember to…"

"Can I start with something to make Mum forget – when I need her to?"

"Forgetting powder, page twenty-five. It is a perfect choice for beginners as you can use ingredients easily found in any well-stocked larder."

Poppy quickly scanned the list then ran downstairs for tea. She had to wait until Mum was putting Jake to bed before she could sneak into the kitchen and get what she needed for the forgetting spell. Back in her bedroom she carefully lit the candle, something she wasn't allowed to do, really, but the book said she couldn't do magic without it. Once it was burning brightly, Poppy measured out flour, baking powder, and a pinch of rosemary.

"Yramesor," she murmured as she stirred. The candle flickered sending shadows leaping over the walls. The powder spun and spiralled upwards. "Done," Poppy cried, remembering just in time to trap the spell in a plastic bag.

"I'VE DONE MY first bit of magic," Poppy told Amelia as they walked to school the next morning.

"Did it work?"

"I don't know. I haven't tried it on anyone yet."

When they reached the school gates a car with darkened windows drew up and a girl wearing sunglasses climbed out. She had very pale skin and dark hair tied into plaits.

"That's weird," Poppy said. "Sunglasses in September when it's so grey and cloudy."

As if she'd heard what Poppy said the girl took off her glasses and stuffed them in her bag. She didn't come into the schoolyard but stood looking around as if she was not quite sure what to do next.

"She looks a bit lost. Shall we go and see if she needs any help?" Amelia said.

"Okay." Poppy linked her friend's arm and they wandered across.

They told the girl their names and Amelia asked if she was new.

The girl nodded and said, "I'm Mia. I'm in 7C."

"That's our class. You can come in with us," Poppy said. Mia did not move.

"It's all right, we don't bite," Amelia said.

"Oh!" Mia turned even paler than before. "You don't?"

"Course not. It's something my dad says as a joke. It's supposed to make you feel better and, um— Trust us."

Mia opened her mouth but before she could say anything the bell rang. Poppy and Amelia pulled faces as Miss Mortimer, the teacher on duty, blew her whistle and ordered everyone to line up. Miss Mortimer was very tall and thin, with short dark hair, a beaky nose, and eyes as hard as pebbles. Everyone was scared of her and they got into their lines very quickly.

Because they'd been talking to Mia, Poppy and Amelia were the last to join their class.

"Just a minute, girls," Miss Mortimer said as they filed past. "I want a word with you."

Are we in trouble? Poppy thought.

We haven't done anything wrong, Amelia's voice sounded in her head. Poppy frowned and put her hand up to her ear. Was she hearing things?

"I believe that you might have certain talents that need to be explored." Miss Mortimer smiled a strange wintery smile that gave Poppy the shivers. "Starting next week you are to attend my Wednesday-after-school club."

"But—" Amelia began.

"What do we have to do?" Poppy was puzzled.

"I will teach you the secrets of the left-hand way. We will explore the paths of mystery and power…" Miss Mortimer's voice was so calm and soothing that Poppy found she was nodding her head.

No! Amelia's voice broke through her thoughts. *Blank her out Poppy. Don't do what she says. Think of nothing, think of greyness, of—*

"Porridge," Poppy said out loud, remembering the boring breakfast she'd had that morning.

Miss Mortimer frowned. "Pardon?"

"Sorry, miss. I wasn't concentrating."

"I see," Miss Mortimer said sharply. "I must have been wrong about you both. You are not the exceptional pupils I thought you were, just two silly girls. Off you go."

What was that all about? Poppy thought as they hurried into the building.

No idea, but it gave me a bad feeling, Amelia replied. "Poppy." Amelia came to a stop in the middle of the corridor. "You know what we're doing?"

"Yes. We're mind messaging." Poppy grinned. "Awesome!"

"Absolutely awesome! I never knew we could do that. It must be cos we're—"

Don't say it, Amelia messaged and they both looked at Mia who was watching them with a puzzled expression on her face.

Chapter 4

"DO YOU WANT to come to my house and try out some spells?" Poppy asked Amelia at the end of the last lesson.

"What about Mia?"

"We can't ask her she's not a—"

Amelia put her finger to her lips but Mia had heard them and was walking away. Her head bowed, shoulders slumped, she went to the door that led out into the schoolyard. When she got there she stopped and looked around as if she was afraid to leave the building.

"Look what you've done," Amelia said.

"I didn't mean to." Poppy felt terrible. "I didn't think she could hear us."

"Well she did." Amelia ran up to Mia. "Poppy didn't mean it like that. She wasn't leaving you out it's just that—"

"It's a project we're doing together." Poppy joined them.

"It's all right. I'm used to it." Mia stared straight in front of her. "My parents move around a lot and it happens in every school I've ever been to. Everyone thinks I'm weird and no one wants to be friends."

"We don't think you're weird. At least—" Poppy glanced at Amelia "—you're no more weird than us."

"You might be a bit pale and—" Amelia stopped.

And you never seem to smile, Poppy thought.

That might be because she's sad, Amelia messaged back.

They turned to Mia.

"You can walk home with us … if you like," Poppy said.

"That's if no one's picking you up," Amelia added.

We can do the spells another time.

The three girls walked out across the yard. Mia seemed more and more nervous but neither Poppy nor Amelia could see why. No other pupil had said or done anything mean. Most were too busy talking to their friends to bother about three Year Seven girls.

When they reached the school gates Mia stopped. She glanced from side to side, listened intently, then shook her head and let out a deep breath.

"It's not here." Her lips curved into a half-smile. "I thought it might be following me but it's not."

"What are you scared of?" Poppy asked.

"Nothing. I don't like dogs, that's all."

"You'll like Bernard. He's a sausage dog and

he's really cute," Amelia said.

"He's a dachshund. He gets upset if you call him a sausage," Poppy said.

"I didn't think dogs could get upset," Mia said.

"Bernard is very sensitive. He's—" Poppy stopped as a huge black dog came bounding towards them. Its eyes were glowing red, its teeth were yellow and pointed and it was getting closer and closer.

"Run," Mia shouted.

Poppy, Amelia and Mia ran. They raced along the road as fast as they could until Mia dodged into a back alley. It was overgrown with weeds and brambles so they ran in single file but it looked as if they had escaped.

"Has it gone?" Poppy panted.

"I think so," Amelia began. "Oh no! Look."

Where there had been one dog, now there were two, one at each end of the alleyway.

"We're trapped," Poppy cried.

"No we're not," Mia said. "Quick. Take my hand. Close your eyes and hold tight."

There was a sudden rush of air. A feeling like going up in a swing then coming right down again, and when Poppy opened her eyes she, Amelia and Mia were in a back garden. Staring at them through the kitchen door was a boy from their class.

"You flew over the wall," Will shouted, running out into the garden.

"Sorry. The vampire dogs were chasing us."

"The what?" The other three stared at Mia.

"Oh!" She put her hands over her mouth. "I shouldn't have said that. Only you weren't supposed to be able to see them and—"

"I didn't see any dogs," Will said.

"No you wouldn't," Amelia sighed.

Because he's not a witch, Poppy messaged. "Will, is it all right if we go out through your house?" she asked.

"Of course it is but first I want to know how you did it."

"I'll tell you later."

Mia gasped. Amelia shook her head. But Poppy ignored them.

"It was weird seeing you appear like that." Will opened the front door to let the girls out into the street.

"You won't tell anyone?" Amelia said.

"Only if you explain, like you said you would."

"I won't forget." Poppy reached into her pocket and took a pinch of forgetting powder from the bag. *But you will.* "Yramesor," she murmured and waved her hand in Will's direction.

A shimmer of silver hung in the air then Will said, "Hi. I didn't know you walked past my house on the way home."

"We don't usually but today we thought we'd try a different route." Poppy linked arms with Mia and Amelia and the three of them walked off down the street.

At the corner Poppy gave the other two some of the forgetting powder. "In case those dogs turn up again. I don't know if it works on animals but it might."

Amelia turned to Mia. "Now we're safe you can tell us what this is all about."

"I can't. I really can't." Mia's eyes were full of tears. "If I do I'll never be able to come to school again. We'll have to move and… Sorry." Before they could do or say anything Mia was gone.

Chapter 5

POPPY AND AMELIA sat on Poppy's bedroom floor with *The Witches' Handbook* open between them. The curtains were drawn and the only light in the room came from a single candle. They were staring intently into a bowl of water.

"I can't see anything," Poppy complained.

"That's cos you're not concentrating." Amelia lifted the candle so they could see the flame flickering on the surface. "If you want to find out where Mia lives you've got to think of her and blank your mind to everything else."

Poppy drew in a deep breath, then slowly breathed out again. The water in the bowl wavered and she saw an old house with turrets, tall windows, and a black door with the number thirty-four on it. She blinked and the vision vanished.

"I know where that is," Poppy said.

"So do I and it won't take long to get there. We can tell your Mum we're going to a friend's, which is true cos Mia is our friend."

THERE WAS A single streetlamp at the start of Mia's road and no lights at all in the house with the turrets. They tried knocking at the front door. They tried at the back. No one answered.

"This is weird," Poppy said.

"It's definitely the right house." Amelia frowned. "Do you think something's happened to Mia?"

"I don't know but I'm going to find out."

"How are you going to do that?"

"We're going down the coal chute." Beside the front door, half-hidden by a bush, was a metal trapdoor.

"It'll be locked," Amelia said.

"Now it isn't." Murmuring an opening spell Poppy clicked her fingers and pointed.

The door was rusty but working together they managed to open it. Poppy clambered through and carefully lowered herself inside. Amelia wasn't sure about breaking into someone's house but she didn't want to be left behind, so she climbed in after Poppy.

At first they thought the cellar was empty. Then Poppy switched on her phone.

"Oh!" she gasped, clutching Amelia's arm.

In the middle of the room were three coffins.

Two large ones and one smaller one.

"That's Mia's, in case you're wondering." A tall white figure with a beard floated through the wall. "I'm Grandpa Ghost and I'm very pleased to meet you." He held out a transparent hand.

"Oh, for goodness sake, Grandpa, remember you're a ghost. I'm Granny." A smaller rounder ghost materialised. "Mia's told us all about you."

"Is she in there?" Poppy hardly dared to point at the coffins.

"Oh no, it's not her bedtime yet," Granny Ghost said.

"So she's a vampire?" Amelia quavered.

"What's wrong with that? Everyone's different. What we look like or where we come from shouldn't make any difference to the way we're treated by other beings."

"Of course not," Poppy said.

"I'm glad we agree about that. If you want to see Mia come with us." The ghosts stepped back through the wall.

"Where do we go?"

"There." Amelia pointed to a door.

The ghosts were waiting at the top of the cellar stairs and showed them into a bright white kitchen where Mia was sitting at the counter doing her homework. "What are you doing here? You shouldn't have come." She glanced over her shoulder.

"Nonsense. They seem perfectly nice girls to

me," said the smaller ghost.

"I know but I'm not allowed visitors – oh no!" Mia jumped to her feet as her parents came in. "I'm sorry, I didn't invite them. They just turned up."

"We came to see if Mia was all right," Poppy explained.

"That's very kind of you. My name is Hera and this is Chris – and yes, we're vampires." Mia's mum smiled revealing sharp pointed fangs. "Don't look so worried. You're quite safe. We don't drink fresh blood in this house."

"We get our supplies from the blood bank." Chris held out his hand. Amelia shrank back but Poppy was determined not to be afraid and shook hands.

"You don't feel any different," she said in surprise.

"We do a pretty good job of blending in."

"Except at school." Mia sat down and put her elbows on the counter and rested her chin on her hands.

"That's because you're new. You have to give it a while before you settle in."

"I don't want it to be like the last time," Mia said miserably.

"That was unfortunate but now you've met Poppy and Amelia…" Hera said.

"Yes." Mia sighed. "That's good but…"

She looked so sad that Poppy put her arm

around her shoulders. "We don't mind what you are. Do we Amelia?"

"Of course not."

"I mind what I am and so do Chris and Hera." Mia looked up at her parents. "I don't want to be like this anymore. I want to be like everyone else."

"Hmm," Poppy said.

"Being like everyone else is boring," Amelia added.

"I don't care. When I grow up I don't want to have to work at night or sleep in a coffin all day and never be able to eat proper food. There's so many things I can't do that my mum and dad did when they were my age."

"Weren't you always vampires then?" Amelia asked.

"No we weren't. It happened just before Mia was born, when we were on holiday in Transylvania," Hera said.

"We got caught in a storm." Chris took up the story. "Our hire car broke down and we went to get shelter in a castle. Unfortunately it turned out to be the home of a very hungry vampire."

"We hoped our baby would be okay but she wasn't."

"So I'm stuck like this," Mia muttered.

"We feel really bad about it," said Hera. "Which is why we thought going to school might help, at least for now."

"But it never works," Mia scowled. "Every

school I go to something goes wrong and we have to move."

"You won't have to this time. We won't tell anyone about you. We promise," Poppy said.

Chris smiled at her. "That's good to know. But we still have to deal with the vampire dogs. They seek out vampires that don't conform. The High Council doesn't like any of us attempting to live like humans."

"They simply refuse to move with the times. They want us all to go back to sucking blood, like in the past," Hera said.

"It's as if they've never heard of the internet or working from home, or mobiles, or even dark glasses," Chris added.

"What happens if the dogs get you?" Amelia asked.

The three vampires shuddered. The ghosts moaned and wailed.

"You don't want to know." Hera shook her head. "As Chris said, now they've found us we could be in big trouble."

"I think we can help."

"You?" Mia's parents stared at Poppy. "How?"

"I've got this spell—"

"They're witches," Mia interrupted. "I did try to tell you. That's why they could see the dogs and why they helped me."

"Whee! Whoo! They've got a spell. We won't have to leave here. We'll be safe!" Granny and

Grandpa Ghost swirled around the room. Chris and Hera smiled. Mia raised her eyes to the ceiling.

"Parents! Ghosts!" she mouthed.

Chapter 6

"IT'S REALLY HARD for Mia, being a vampire," Poppy said when she called for Amelia the next day. "So I had this idea—"

"Poppy—" Amelia sniffed then wrinkled her nose "—you stink."

"It's the garlic paste sandwiches."

"What?" Amelia waved her hand in front of her face and moved to the edge of the pavement.

"They're not for me. They're for Mia."

"Won't they make her shrivel up … or something?"

"Not if she only has a tiny bite. I thought they might work like a vaccine. You know, to inoculate her against being a vampire."

"Can you do that?"

"I don't know. We can try."

Mia was waiting for them at the school gates. She came to greet them then stepped back quickly when she moved too close to Poppy.

"I can't," she said after Poppy explained her plan.

"That's okay. I'll throw them in the bin." Poppy was disappointed but she understood that Mia might not want to risk crumbling into dust.

"No wait. If it means I could—" Mia looked longingly at Amelia's backpack "—eat cheese and onion crisps…"

"They're my favourite," Amelia said.

"Mine too. Or they would be, if I could eat them."

"So do you want to try my idea?" Poppy broke a tiny piece off a sandwich and held it out on the palm of her hand.

Mia looked at it as if it was something that had crawled out from under a stone. Then holding the garlic paste sandwich with the tips of her fingers she lifted it to her lips.

What if she's allergic? What if she goes into shock? Do epi-pens work on vampires? Amelia messaged frantically.

I don't know. Poppy's eyes were fixed on Mia as the vampire girl sunk her teeth into the bread. Her mouth closed. She chewed. She swallowed.

Poppy and Amelia held their breath.

Mia swayed and shuddered. She gasped and moaned.

What do we do? Poppy thought.

"That wasn't—" Mia's face twisted in distaste "—that bad."

"You don't even smell of garlic." Amelia sniffed in Mia's direction.

"That's cos she didn't have very much."

"It was enough." Mia grimaced. She turned to Poppy. "Only it wasn't, was it?"

"No. Sorry. It was only the first dose."

"You mean I have to take more?"

"Yes. Until we know it's worked." Poppy looked at Mia, expecting her to say no.

"I'll give it a try," Mia said. "Now what about those vampire dogs?"

AT THE END of the day as the three girls were leaving school they stopped at the gates. Mia looked up and down the crowded street.

"I can't see them."

"Maybe they've given up," Amelia said hopefully.

"No wait. Look over there." Poppy pointed across the road where weaving in and out of the groups of school kids were two big black dogs. Invisible to everyone else, they padded purposefully towards the three girls. "You know what to do, don't you?"

Mia drew in her breath and nodded. "I'm scared," she whispered, but Poppy and Amelia were already racing towards the alleyway. Keeping her eyes on the dogs, Mia counted to fifty then followed. Eager for the hunt, the hounds lifted their heads, gave a blood-curdling howl, and charged after her.

Mia dodged past a mum with a double buggy and an old lady on a mobility scooter. She almost tripped over a small hairy dog that was whining and barking and turning in circles around its master's legs.

"Don't know what's got into you," the man was saying.

A pair of slavering blood-sucking vampire dogs, Mia thought.

She was almost there. A few more paces and she'd be at the entrance to the alleyway. She could hear the snapping and snarling coming closer. One final sprint and —

— a street cleaning cart was blocking her way.

Hoping the driver wouldn't see her Mia sprang. Over the top of the cart she sailed and landed feet first in the alley. A thud and a thump told her that one of the dogs was behind her. Trying not to show how scared she was, Mia backed away.

The dog growled. It bared its teeth and prepared to attack.

"Here!" Poppy stepped out of her hiding place. Distracted, the dog turned as she threw a handful of forgetting powder at it. The animal shook its head and looked around as if wondering what it was doing there. Then it cocked its leg against an old mattress and trotted to the other end of the alley where its companion was looking equally bewildered.

"It worked!" Amelia cried. "I got the other dog with my forgetting powder."

"Which means Chris, Hera and me, we're all safe."

"You won't have to leave school and go somewhere else." Poppy lifted her hand and they all gave each other a high five.

Chapter 7

"I WANT TO fly like Mia," Poppy said as she and Amelia walked home. "It'll be awesome. All we need is broomsticks."

"I'm not sure—" Amelia began but Poppy ignored her.

"They'll have to be special ones, but where do we get them?"

"We could ask Mrs Harrison," Amelia suggested, hoping that was enough to change Poppy's mind. "But I don't think we're ready."

"Course we are. Flying's what witches do and since Mrs Harrison said we're not to bother her unless we absolutely have to, we'll do it on our own. Come back to my house and we'll look in the handbook."

Amelia shrugged. The idea of being up in the sky perched on a piece of wood and a few twigs scared her but if it was part of being a witch perhaps it was something she would have to try. She was very relieved when they got to Poppy's bedroom because for once the handbook had nothing useful to say.

"I'm not a street directory," it told them huffily and shut with a bang.

Poppy, however, wasn't going to give up. After Mum finished her work she let them borrow her laptop. The two girls sat on Poppy's bed and scrolled down the screen. "This isn't working," Poppy grumbled. "I can't find anything. No wait, I'll do what you said and…" She closed her eyes and conjured up an image of a broomstick flying across a starlit sky.

Lights fizzed across the screen. Jagged streaks of ruby, emerald and indigo zigged and zagged, then merged into a deep purple colour. Spidery, silver letters spread across the page, and Poppy read, "The Witches' Emporium: a wondrous place for all your magical requirements. Broomsticks a speciality. Number 13 Lime Road. Open Fridays only, from midnight until the break of day."

"Yes," Poppy breathed, "that's where we have to go."

Amelia looked doubtful. "In the middle of the night? And what about money. How are we going to pay for these broomsticks?"

Poppy looked at the screen. "Ducats, guineas, florins and witchgeld only. Witches', Warlocks' and Wizards' credit cards also accepted."

"We can't go. We don't have any of those," Amelia said happily.

"We don't, but we know someone who does."

"Not Mrs Harrison! I thought you said we were going to do this on our own."

"We are but we can't get broomsticks without

the right money."

"Do we have to?"

"If we want to fly, we do. What's the point of being a witch if you can't? Besides, Mrs Harrison did say we could come back any time if we *really* needed to."

"Mm." Amelia was unconvinced. She was still not sure the next day, and after the bell rang for the end of school Amelia was the last to leave the classroom.

"Did you tell your dad you're going to be late?" Poppy asked. Amelia nodded miserably.

"It's all right. If he says anything, we'll sprinkle some forgetting powder when we get back," Poppy tried to reassure her.

Amelia looked past her to where Mia was walking away down the road. *Wish I was going home,* she thought.

Well, we're not, Poppy messaged back.

I didn't mean to send that.

Okay, but if you really don't want to I'll go on my own.

There was a long pause. Amelia blanked her mind and stared straight in front of her. Poppy was beginning to think her friend had given up on the whole idea when Amelia said, "I'm coming with you."

And Poppy breathed a sigh of relief.

LABURNUM AVENUE WAS every bit as dark and gloomy as they remembered – and a bit more. The hedges seemed higher, the lights dimmer, the road longer. There was no sign of the black iron gates or the yellow car, and Poppy and Amelia were soon beginning to wonder if they would ever find the rambling cottage where the Harrisons lived. "We must have got it wrong. It's not here," Amelia said.

"That's because they've hidden it. I read about it in *The Witches' Handbook*. You can put a glamour on something and no one can see it unless you want them to."

"Then Mrs Harrison doesn't want to see us. Come on Poppy, let's go home."

"And give up being proper witches? No way. You can if you want but I'm—" She grabbed Amelia's arm. "Look, there's Marmaduke."

The marmalade cat sauntered down the pavement towards them. Purring loudly, he twisted and twined around their legs and suddenly the two girls could see the pair of black iron gates with a glimpse of a yellow car beyond, and a cottage with a roof like a frown.

Without waiting for her friend, Poppy set off. Amelia hesitated for a moment then followed.

Marmaduke gave a sharp mew and with his tail held up like a question mark he trotted to the back of the cottage, leapt onto the workroom window and tapped it with his paw. A line of light appeared around the door. The handle glowed and as Poppy touched it the door swung open.

"Yes?" Mrs Harrison was standing at her workbench, a vial of purple liquid in her hand.

"We've come about broomsticks," Poppy said.

"Ah!" Mrs Harrison said in a voice that could have been angry or surprised.

Unsure which it was, Poppy looked at Amelia. Amelia looked at Poppy. Neither girl said anything.

Mrs Harrison gave them a sharp look. "Are you ready for flying?"

"Yes," said Poppy.

"No," said Amelia.

"Make up your minds. Hesitation is a bad habit for a witch. Decision is what is required."

Poppy took a deep breath. "We want to buy some broomsticks. Don't we?" She looked at Amelia who nodded reluctantly.

"Suppose so. I mean … yes, okay. I'll give it a go," said Amelia.

"Hmm." Mrs Harrison blew down her nose in a disapproving manner. "It's true that if you are serious about your magic then you must learn to fly."

Did Mr Harrison? Amelia thought.

"My son was a disappointment in that department. He is totally unsuited to a life of witchcraft."

"Sorry." Amelia apologised out loud. "I was only thinking—"

"Then don't. You must learn to shield your thoughts. Especially in the presence of other magical beings. Back to the matter of broomsticks. Every witch must source her own broom."

"We've done that," Poppy broke in. "We can get them from the Witches' Emporium on Friday, only we don't have any witchgeld."

"So you came here hoping I would give you some."

Poppy flushed. To her surprise it was Amelia who said, "We came to ask you what to do. You did say we could, if we were stuck…" Her voice trailed off.

"I did," the witch agreed. "That doesn't mean that I will give you what require. If you want witchgeld you will have to work for it."

See what you got us into, Amelia flashed the message before she could stop.

To her relief Mrs Harrison ignored it. "Witchgeld must be earned, otherwise it will not buy what you want."

"What do we have to do?" Poppy was eager to start.

"Your task is to wash, dry and polish every vial and potion bottle." Mrs Harrison pointed to the row upon row of glassware that filled the shelves on every wall.

"But they're full of spells."

"Ah!" Mrs Harrison smiled a not very pleasant smile. "That does make it more difficult, but I'm sure you'll manage. Come along, Marmaduke. Let's leave the apprentice witches to their task." The marmalade cat gave them an encouraging mew then turned and followed his mistress out of the room.

"We'll never get this done before morning," Poppy groaned.

"We will if we start now." Amelia walked over to the sink, turned on the taps and squirted washing up liquid into the water. A line of bubbles formed on the surface.

"That's no good. We haven't got time to wash every single bottle."

"Then you think of something." Amelia glared at her friend. "You got us into this. You get us out."

"You agreed."

"I didn't."

"Oh no?"

As their voices rose, so did the bubbles. They grew bigger and bigger, until they tipped over the edge of the sink and cascaded onto the floor.

"That's it," Poppy said. "A cleaning spell."

"Do you know any?"

"No." Poppy captured a bubble on the end of

her finger and blew. The bubble landed on Amelia's nose. Amelia flicked it off. She put her hands into the sink and scooped up a handful of bubbles and flung them at Poppy. Some landed on her hair, some on her shoulders, and some on her back. Others floated away, upwards and sideways, filling the room with globes of iridescent soapy water. As the bubbles increased in size Poppy was pummelled from side to side and Amelia struggled to stay on her feet. The bottles and vials rattled and shook and one, full of green liquid, teetered to the edge of the shelf.

"Catch it," Poppy cried.

Amelia stretched out her arm. "Conmoro!" she commanded and the bottle stopped in mid-air.

How did you do that? Poppy asked.

I don't know.

Don't let it fall.

I can't hold it much longer. As the thought crossed Amelia's mind the bottle crashed to the floor. Green gunge oozed over the tiles and a smell of damp trees filled the air. Glass clinked and clattered and another bottle was nudged towards the brink.

"Help! There's a bubble on my face. I can't breathe," Amelia cried.

"Pop it, stop it." Poppy banged her fists against her legs. "Cease, desist," she yelled. Bubbles wobbled and quivered. Some deflated, some burst, others sank back into the sink and flowed away down the drain.

"Are you okay?"

"I think so. There's a soapy taste in my mouth but I can breathe again."

"That was scary. But look." Poppy pointed to a row of clean and sparkling bottles. "We were supposed to use the bubbles. Amelia you're a genius."

"I know." Amelia smirked.

"Except we haven't finished."

"I'm not getting bubbles all over me again," Amelia said firmly.

"You don't have to. We can make a spell." Poppy half-closed her eyes and chanted, "Bubble, bubble save us trouble."

"Wash and polish, clean and gleam," Amelia added.

"Bright as sunshine on a stream," they finished together and stepping back they watched as a steady stream of bubbles rose into the air and washed and polished every vial and bottle until they sparkled and shone.

"We did it!" Poppy held up her palm.

"Except for that." Amelia pointed to the green goo on the floor.

"There's got to be a spell for that too." Poppy screwed up her eyes but, however hard she tried, she couldn't think of a single word.

"Nruter." Amelia clicked her fingers. The pieces of broken glass rose from the floor and ground together. The green liquid slurped back into the mended bottle which returned to its place on the shelf.

"How did you do that?"

"I did some homework. That handbook's got lots of useful stuff in it."

"Quite right too. Practice makes progress." Mrs Harrison appeared in the doorway carrying a tray.

She scanned the room with its shelves of gleaming bottles. "You've worked hard and must be tired and hungry. So you can have a snack before you go." She put the tray down on the table.

Poppy was hungry but was eating a witch's food a good idea? She glanced at Amelia.

"It's perfectly safe. I'm not going to turn a pair of promising young witches into toads, am I?" Mrs Harrison looked at them fiercely. Not wanting to make her angry, Poppy and Amelia shook their heads. "Good. Eat your cranberry cookies and drink your blackcurrant fizz."

"So we did all right?" Poppy dared to say through a mouthful of crumbly biscuit.

"Hmm." The witch pursed her lips. "It certainly looks like you've done a good job. Haven't they Marmaduke?"

The cat leapt onto a shelf, ran his tail along a line of bottles and gave a sharp mew.

"You have Marmaduke's seal of approval. He likes to keep everything in order." The cat settled himself in the witch's lap. She stroked his head and he purred contentedly.

Poppy and Amelia shuffled on their seats. Marmaduke nudged the witch's arm.

"I've not forgotten." Mrs Harrison clicked her fingers and two drawstring bags appeared on the tray. "The red one is yours Poppy. The blue one is for Amelia. There's no need to look inside. Each one will contain exactly the right amount of money."

The marmalade cat leapt from her knee. His tail curved and Poppy and Amelia knew it was time to leave.

Chapter 8

AT QUARTER TO midnight everything was ready. A life sized Poppy shape lay sleeping in her bed while the real Poppy Barrington was creeping downstairs and out of the back door, where Amelia was waiting for her in the alleyway. Away from the main road it was dark and Poppy used her phone to light their way past the tangle of brambles, the pile of wooden pallets, a rusty pizza oven, a broken guinea pig hutch, and a heap of empty bottles.

"It'll be so much better when we can fly," she said, kicking aside an empty can.

"We could get rid of all the rubbish. We could make it into a witch's garden. I was reading about all the herbs you can use for spells and..." Amelia was in no hurry to get to the Witches' Emporium.

"We'll do that later." Poppy was getting impatient. "Right now we're going shopping."

Number 13 Lime Road looked exactly the same as all the other houses in the street until Poppy and Amelia opened the gate and stepped onto the path. At that moment the words **The Witches' Emporium** appeared in black letters on the frosted glass above the purple door. The knocker was in the shape of a witch with her cat on a broomstick.

When Poppy touched it a voice said, "Knock three times, then enter your password."

"Oh no!" Poppy wailed. "It didn't say anything about a password."

"Maybe that's something we're supposed to know."

"I don't see how." Poppy scowled at the door. They'd worked so hard to get to this point and now it looked as if it was all going to be for nothing.

"*The Witches' Handbook* might have something that—" Amelia began.

"Password correct," said a voice. "Knock thrice and enter."

Poppy did as she was told. The door swung open and they stepped inside. Fairy lights were strung along the walls and spiders' webs, sparkling with glitter, dangled from the ceiling which glowed with a sprinkle of stars and moons.

"Welcome." A plump witch with pink hair and lace-up boots trotted towards them. "I'm Marigold Merryfeather and I'm here to show you around. In the front room—" she opened the door "—we have spells and enchantments of all sorts. If you want someone to fall in love with you we have love spells. If you want someone to fall out of love with you then we have falling-out spells. Then there are amulets, milagros, scarabs and four-leafed clovers for luck. Is there anything in particular you are looking for? Whatever it is we are bound to have it."

"We haven't come for spells, thank you," Poppy said.

"Oh, cats and candlesticks! There I go again. Talking too much is my great weakness. If you are looking for crystal balls then you will find what you need in the next room. Then there are—"

"Broomsticks?" Poppy prompted.

"They're our speciality, as it says on the website and in the brochure. You do have a brochure?" The girls shook their heads. "Never mind, take one, take two, take as many as you like and give them to all the witches you know."

"We don't know any, expect for Mrs Harrison," Amelia said.

"Fedora Harrison. How wonderful! A great friend of mine. I've known her for centuries, ever since…"

Poppy looked at Amelia. Amelia shook her head. At this rate they wouldn't even see a broomstick let alone choose one before daybreak.

"Excuse me, but we don't have much time," Poppy said.

"Of course and if you came for a broomstick, a broomstick you shall have." The witch smiled happily. "Come along. We keep them in the back bedroom." Still talking, Marigold set off up the stairs. "Some of our customers like to go for a test flight and it's simpler to fly out of an upstairs window. There's less chance of anyone catching an unfortunate glimpse of things they shouldn't see. Mind the toad, as you go. He does like to sit on the landing and it's so easy to trip over him. I sometimes think—" she lowered her voice as if letting them into a secret "—that he does it on purpose. He's not the best tempered creature I've ever had." The toad gave them a long yellow-eyed glare and Amelia, remembering what it was like to be turned into an amphibian, shivered.

"He's not … he didn't used to be … human, did he?" she whispered.

"Oh no! Well maybe, once upon a time. But he's happy as he is."

"How do you know?" Poppy asked.

"Because he's my familiar. All witches have them, though I suppose as you've only just started along the path that you haven't reached that stage yet. Hop along Horatio—" she waved her hand at the toad "—these girls have come for broomsticks. How exciting is that?"

Horatio shot her a withering look and hopped heavily to the side of the stairs.

Poppy and Amelia hurried past him. Marigold flung open a door and announced, "Here we have our world-renowned broomstick department. Step inside and pick your broom of choice. We have everything from the advanced models – super speed and special features being standard – to those for beginners." She gestured to a rack of brooms on the righthand side of the room. "Which will be what you are looking for."

"Yes please." Poppy ran over to the beginners' brooms. Amelia bit her lip and stayed close to the door.

"Oh dear no!" Marigold threw up her hands. "That's not how it's done. You have to let the broom choose you."

Amelia took another step back so that she was almost out in the corridor. As she did so one of the brooms shook itself, rustled its twigs, and flew across the room towards her.

"Put your hand up and prepare to receive your broomstick," Marigold said calmly and Amelia did as she was told. The feel of the wood against her palm made her skin tingle. The broom gave a contented sigh and Amelia's fingers closed around it.

"There!" the witch beamed. "That's you sorted. A happy broom makes for a happy customer and a happy customer is a happy witch. Now for your friend. Let's see which one has chosen her."

Not a single broom moved. Not a twig twitched. Poppy's shoulders slumped. It was like being left out in a games lesson after everyone else had been chosen for a team. Did this mean she'd never be a proper witch?

"Don't worry." Marigold put a comforting hand on her shoulder. "It can take time for a broom to make up its mind. They're very fussy, you know."

Poppy stared at the rack of brooms and tried not to panic.

It'll be all right, Amelia messaged. *I don't mind sharing. If you don't get one of your own you can always have a lift on mine.*

Before Poppy could reply the brooms shifted and shuffled like people elbowing their way out of a crowd. Then they leaned in together and made a shape like a wigwam.

"Cats and candlesticks! I've never seen them do that before." Marigold clasped her hands.

"I've never had my own broomstick before," Poppy said happily as one shot out of the top of the wigwam and flew towards her.

"Catch it!" Amelia cried but the broom was already in Poppy's hand, wriggling helpfully as she adjusted her grip.

"Hello broomstick," Poppy said. The wriggling stopped. "I think it likes me."

"Of course it does or it wouldn't have come to you. Now that you are both happy customers…" The pink-haired witch held out her hand. Poppy gave her the red drawstring bag. Marigold weighed it on her palm and nodded. "Exactly right, thank you." Amelia did the same with the blue bag.

Holding tightly onto their broomsticks the two girls followed Marigold Merryfeather down the stairs.

"Before you go, there are a couple of things you need to know. First, a broomstick is for life not just for Halloween. It will decide when it needs to be retired, but in the meantime it will upgrade itself as your flying skills improve. Secondly, only you and other witches can see your broomsticks. This means that you can take them with you wherever you go. Personally, I find that very useful because you never know when you might have an emergency, and if you do, being able to make a quick exit can be invaluable. I think that's all I've got to tell you. Do either of you have any questions before you go? No?"

Poppy shook her head. Amelia frowned and said hesitantly, "Can we have lessons?"

"Flying lessons?" Marigold looked so surprised that Amelia, afraid that she'd said something stupid, blushed and looked down at her feet.

"Oh, you don't need to worry about that. For most witches flying comes naturally. True, others have more difficulty but I'm sure you'll both manage fine. Lovely to meet you. Goodbye." She waved her hand.

Even though they were nowhere near it, the door opened and Poppy and Amelia found themselves out in the street standing in front of a perfectly ordinary house with no sign whatsoever that it was also the Witches' Emporium.

"Let's fly home." Poppy was bubbling with excitement.

"You can if you like. I'm walking."

"Scaredy cat," Poppy taunted, but deep down she was relieved that the first flight on her broomstick was not going to be down Lime Road in the middle of the night.

Chapter 9

MEET YOU ON *The Downs. Bring broomstick and we can practice flying,* Poppy messaged. There was no reply and she thought she was going to have to go on her own when the doorbell rang and there was Amelia clutching her broomstick in one hand and a cycling helmet in the other.

"What did you bring that for?" Poppy asked.

"In case I fall off."

"Well I'm not going to. I'm a natural on a broomstick."

"Oh yeah?" Amelia scoffed. Poppy thumped her on the arm. Amelia responded with a push and they continued joshing about until they reached the wide expanse of open land that was The Downs.

"What if someone sees us?" Amelia asked.

"Well…" Poppy said slowly. "Since people can't fly and only another witch can see our broomsticks they'll think they're seeing things."

"But they might take pictures," Amelia persisted.

"Stop worrying," Poppy exploded. "Who cares if they do? I'm going over there past those trees and then I'm going to fly."

Poppy ran off and Amelia followed slowly, trailing her broomstick behind her. The twigs rustled along the grass. The handle gave a wriggle. *It wants me to get on*, Amelia thought. *Okay broom, if you're ready.* The broomstick bounced up and down. She let go and it rose into the air, where it tilted at an angle and waited. Amelia sat on it and the broomstick glided forward.

"I'm flying!" she yelled.

"Me too!" Poppy didn't want to be left behind even though she was still holding her broomstick upright and it showed no signs of going anywhere. "Come on broom, let's catch her up." The broomstick didn't move. "Oh COME ON!" Poppy was getting cross. Here she was, stuck on the ground while Amelia was racing above The Downs. Round and round she went, soaring up into the air then flying so low that Poppy had to duck as Amelia swooped over the top of her head. "Watch out," Poppy shouted.

"Help!" Amelia wailed. "I can't stop, I can't—" The broomstick accelerated and she was gone, a small speck of a girl on a broom disappearing into the distance.

"Hang on," Poppy cried. "I'm on my way. Broomstick, we've got to follow Amelia. She needs our help." The broomstick did not move. "Please—" Poppy was frantic "—let me fly you." The broomstick rustled its twigs, its handle wriggled, and when Poppy let go it tilted forward and hovered so that she could get on. Poppy held on tight and it wobbled and juddered and rose a few centimetres.

"Can't you go any higher? Please," Poppy pleaded. The broomstick gave a tremendous lurch and reached the height of a small bush. "That's no good. We're never going to find Amelia like this." The broomstick jerked forward and for a few seconds it flew smoothly – then it bumped up and down and began to tip forward.

"Straighten up," Poppy yelled. The stick turned upright and she slid down until her bottom was resting on the twigs and her feet were dragging along the ground. "Stop!" Poppy screamed.

The broomstick stopped. It balanced on its twigs then fell over with a thump, taking Poppy with it. Face down in a clump of grass, mouth full of dirt, Poppy wanted to howl but crying was not going to help Amelia. She spat out some grit and scrambled to her feet. Her knees were bruised and her palms grazed but it didn't feel as if anything was broken.

The broomstick lay motionless on the ground and she felt like kicking it until she remembered that it, like her and Amelia, was new to flying. "Okay, I'm not as good as I thought I'd be," she admitted, picking up the broom and dusting it off. "But we still have to find Amelia. And I don't know where to start."

Her phone pinged and she saw she had a text from Mia. *Hi, where are you? What are you doing? I'm so bored. Want to meet up?*

"Yes!" Poppy punched the air. This could be the solution.

I'm on The Downs. We need help.

Before Poppy put her phone back in her pocket Mia was standing beside her.

"Where's Amelia?"

"Her broomstick took off. Mine isn't working and I can't go and look for her."

"I'll help." Mia held out her hand.

"I don't know where she is."

"Then message her."

Poppy felt stupid for not having thought of that. She closed her eyes and concentrated as hard as she could. At first there was nothing, then Amelia messaged, *I'm at the top of the tower in Blaise Woods.*

Can you get down?

It's too high up. I fell off and the broomstick left me here.

Mia and I are on our way.

"I've found her." Poppy picked up her broomstick.

"What are you doing with that? If you're coming with me, you don't need it," Mia said.

"I can't leave it behind. It's like swans or something. I'm stuck with it for life." Poppy gave the broom a shake and took the vampire girl's hand. Mia gave her a reassuring wink and leapt into the air.

Up and up they rose, rising high above The Downs. The wind pressed against their faces and the landscape far beneath them began to blur.

Poppy had that feeling in her stomach, the kind you get when a lift is going down too fast. She was about to ask Mia to slow down when, without any warning, she was standing on the top of a stone tower at the centre of a dark wood.

Sitting with her back against the battlements, her arms around her knees, was Amelia.

"I tried to get down but the door's locked." Amelia was almost crying. "My phone isn't working and I shouted and shouted but there's no one around. I thought I was going to be stuck here for ever."

"We've come to find you and rescue you." Mia stretched out her hand.

Amelia took a deep breath. "I can't. I'm scared."

"You let me fly you over the wall when the vampire dogs were after us."

"That was different. Can't you go and get help? Fly down to the museum and ask them for the key."

"How are we going to explain how you got up here?" Poppy said.

"I hadn't thought of that. I just want to go home."

"You will but we have to do it on our own

otherwise there'll be all sorts of trouble. No one will believe us if we tell them what really happened. You've got to let me help you."

"Okay." Amelia took Mia's hand. Poppy took the other and held on tight. She waited for the upward rush but nothing happened.

"Sorry. I'm a bit tired. I've never gone so far before. At least not with someone else," Mia said.

"And this time there's me and Amelia. If we're too much for you, we'll have to…" Poppy looked at her broomstick. "Please, can you, will you, would you…?" The broomstick rustled its twigs. "You'll try?" The broomstick wriggled. Poppy gulped. It was a long way down to the ground and even further to get home, but if that was the only way of rescuing Amelia then she was going to have to do it.

"Amelia, hold on tight," Poppy said as the broomstick made itself ready.

"I can't," Amelia wailed.

"You've got to," Mia hissed, her lips curling fiercely and for the first time Poppy and Amelia caught a glimpse of sharp white vampire teeth. They looked at each other and back at Mia who grinned.

"It's so high up," Amelia gasped as she climbed on behind Poppy.

"Then don't look," Mia said and with a swoosh she was gone.

"Please broomstick, fly us to the ground,"

Poppy said and very, very slowly the broom rose up above the battlements, hovered for a moment, gave a terrifying wobble, then in a series of jerks and hops, like an airborne kangaroo, it began to descend.

As soon as their feet were on the ground Amelia jumped off, ran to the bushes and was horribly sick. "I'm never, ever, ever going to fly again," she said a few moments later.

"Okay," Poppy gave up. "I'll phone Dad and ask him to pick us up."

Mia shot her a glance to say that was going to ruin everything.

"You don't have to." Some of the colour was coming back into Amelia's cheeks. "There's a bus we can catch. It stops at the park gates and it'll take us home."

"If we had any money," Poppy said sourly. She'd been so excited about being able to fly and now everything was going wrong.

"I've got some," Mia said unexpectedly. "I thought we might go for a hot chocolate at that new burger place. I'm almost ready to try one. Or even one of those smoothie things…" She trailed off.

"You're a star!" Poppy cried and gave her a hug. For a moment Mia did not react and Poppy wondered if she'd done something wrong. Then Mia hugged her back and not wanting to be left out Amelia put her arms around the pair of them.

"No one's ever hugged before," Mia said when they'd let go of each other.

"That's because you've never had friends like us," Poppy said.

It was quite a walk from the tower to the bus stop but at least they didn't have to wait long. Claiming the back seat, Poppy propped her broomstick up in the corner. "Amelia, what's happened to your broom?"

"I don't know and I don't care. After I fell off, it circled around for a bit then it whizzed off."

"It could be anywhere. It could be flying around Bristol for ever," Mia said.

Poppy's broomstick shuddered. "We can't leave it like that. Marigold Merryfeather said a broomstick is not just for Halloween..." She looked at Amelia.

"It's for life," Amelia groaned.

"We have to find it. We have to get it back."

"How are we going to do that?" asked Mia.

Chapter 10

BY THE TIME the bus dropped them off at their stop the daylight was fading and the streetlights were coming on. Mia said goodbye and Poppy and Amelia returned to Poppy's house to see what *The Witches' Handbook* had to say about missing broomsticks.

"There must be a spell we can do to get it back." Poppy took the book off the shelf and shut her bedroom door so that Jake wouldn't come in and disturb them.

"Of course there is. There is always a spell," *The Witches' Handbook* said helpfully. "Management of broomsticks. Let me see, that will be Chapter Four. Though I must say it's rather careless of you to have lost your broom so early in your training."

"It wasn't me." Poppy spoke without thinking.

Amelia blushed and said, "It's mine that's gone missing."

"In that case I suggest you refer to your own handbook. I belong to Poppy Barrington."

"Fine. But Amelia's here and I want to help her so—"

The book heaved an exaggerated sigh, fluttered its pages loudly and fell open.

"Does yours do this?" Poppy asked.

"No." Amelia looked sideways at the book. "Mine's very quiet and polite."

"Humph," said the book.

"Ignore it. Let's see what we have to do," Poppy said. Side by side they read the spell. "It seems easy enough. All you have to do is whistle and it will come back to you."

"I can't whistle. You know I can't."

The book groaned loudly. "Then try a whistling spell. Here, page 508. And while you're about it I suggest you open the window."

"We were going to do that anyway," Poppy said though it hadn't occurred to her. She glared at the book. A corner of the page curled up then flicked flat again.

"That was rude," Amelia said.

The book lay perfectly still.

"I don't think it meant it," Poppy said quickly. With a broomstick that had to be asked nicely if it would let her fly, and a handbook that had a mind of its own, being a witch was more complicated than she'd ever imagined.

"Go on, Amelia, say the words."

"Like the whistling of the wind

Like a kettle on the flame

Whistle, whistle, whistle, come to me," Amelia chanted, then pursed her lips and blew. Not a sound came out. She tried again and managed a faint squeak. "Told you. It's no good."

"Let me try."

"It won't work. It's not your broom."

"It might." Poppy went to the window, put her fingers in her mouth and whistled so loudly that Amelia, who was standing next to her, clapped her hands over her ears.

"It's got to have heard that," Poppy said proudly.

"Can you see anything? Is it coming back?"

Poppy peered out of the window. "Mmm… No," she said at last. "Okay, you were right." She turned to the book which gave a jump of triumph. "What do we do now?"

"I suggest that your friend goes home and consults her own handbook, which may have something useful to say."

"I've got a better idea. If all Amelia has to do is whistle… Wait there."

Poppy ran downstairs and came back with Bernard's dog whistle.

"Try that. If the book is right—" there was an offended *hrrumph* from the book "—it'll work."

Amelia took the whistle and blew. Both girls waited, scanning the sky for the returning broomstick. "Told you," Amelia said when nothing happened.

"Do it again. Only louder."

Amelia took a deep breath and blew an ear shattering, brain-riveting blast. In the kitchen, Bernard dived into his basket and stuck his head under the blanket, while over the roofs and chimneypots like a rocket aiming at the moon came Amelia's broomstick.

"Get down!" Poppy yelled and both girls ducked as it flew in straight over their heads and did a few laps around the room before coming to a halt in front of Amelia, where it stood trembling as if it knew it had not behaved itself.

"It's all right. It wasn't your fault. I'm not very good at riding, that's all," Amelia said.

"May I suggest—" the book broke in "—that you have flying lessons, as mentioned in Chapter Four, The Management of Broomsticks."

"That is what we're going to do, thank you." Poppy shut the book and put it back in its place on the shelf.

"Only saying," came a muffled voice.

"Does it ever shut up?" Amelia asked.

There was an annoyed shuffling sound and one of the other books crashed to the ground.

"Only when it's not cross, which is some – I mean most of the time."

As Poppy leaned over to pick up the fallen copy of *City of Secrets* a large red leaf floated in through the window. On it was written in black spiky letters, **Flying Broomstick Academy. Lessons on The Downs. Midnight.**

"Does it always have to be in the middle of the night?" Amelia sighed.

"It's the witching hour," the book muttered.

"Any more comments and I'm going to shove you under the stairs," Poppy said.

"Or you could put a shutting up spell on it," Amelia suggested and after that the book stayed silent.

Chapter 11

IT WAS HARD staying awake till midnight. Poppy's bed was warm and cosy and when she tried to read her eyes kept closing. What she needed was a staying-awake spell.

"Page 208," the book said as soon as she opened it. "Don't make too much noise about it will you." It yawned loudly.

"Ginseng, ginger and chilli. It sounds like a recipe."

"Spells are recipes," the book said sleepily and snapped shut.

"Wait a minute I need to check—" Poppy began then changed her mind. There was no time to deal with a cross and tired book and she was almost sure she could remember exactly how much of each ingredient she needed.

Luckily, all the spices were in the cupboard. She measured them out and took the cup back to her bedroom. "Bang, crash, smash, ring, ding, sing," she chanted and threw a handful of powder into the air. "No sleeping, no dreaming, keep me awake till morning. Atishoo!" Poppy sneezed and sneezed and went on sneezing until the powder settled and her nose stopped itching and her eyes stopped streaming.

I'm outside. I've been waiting for ages Amelia messaged. Poppy grabbed her broom and the largest handkerchief she could find and crept down the stairs. At the very bottom there was a faint *wuff*.

"It's all right Bernard, it's only me," Poppy whispered. The *wuff* became a snuffle and then a snore. She put the handkerchief over her mouth and nose and made a dash for the door.

Amelia was sitting on the wall outside. She looked very pale and was chewing her nails. "I'm not flying there." She glared at the broomstick propped up beside her. "I'm not getting on this thing until I know how to do it properly."

"Right," Poppy said slowly, trying not to sound cross. "We can't walk to The Downs in the middle of the night so you'll have to ride with me, like we did at Blaise Castle. It's the only way we're going to get there." Amelia looked more and more doubtful. "Broomstick, please will you take me and Amelia and her broom to our flying lesson?"

Poppy's broomstick rustled its twigs then leaned forward and hovered horizontally, so the girls could get on. "It's like riding a bike," Poppy said encouragingly.

"No it isn't." Holding her broomstick in one hand, Amelia's other arm went round Poppy's waist and she clung on tight as they rose jerkily into the air.

I hope no one can see us, Poppy thought as the two girls skimmed along the pavement. She was not sure whether they were too heavy for the broomstick, whether it was being kind to Amelia by not flying too high … or it simply didn't know what it was doing.

My feet are almost touching the ground Amelia messaged.

Told you it would be okay, Poppy replied. *If we manage to get up the hill.*

And our bottoms don't scrape the pavement. Amelia's giggles tickled the back of Poppy's neck and she laughed so much she almost fell off. The broomstick lurched crossly.

"Sorry," Poppy said to the broomstick. "You're doing really well." The broom shook itself then glided smoothly onward. It even managed the steep incline up to The Downs, though by the time they reached the top it was flying so close to the ground that they had to pull their knees up to stop their feet snagging on the grass.

"Get ready to land," Poppy warned. The broomstick dropped down and they jumped clear. Brooms in hand, she and Amelia looked around for any sign of the Flying Broomstick Academy. They couldn't see anyone but Poppy's broom bounced up and down then pulled to the left.

"I think it knows where to go," Poppy said and the broom steered them safely past any dips and hollows until they arrived at a stretch of flat ground where a group of girls of about their own age was waiting.

"Ah, Poppy and Amelia, here you are." A young witch with a clipboard came to greet them. "I am Miss Hyacinth and now that we are all present we can begin."

"I think we should introduce ourselves first." A tall girl with a ponytail stepped forward. "I'm Vivica," she announced loudly. "This is—" She turned to the girl next to her.

"Primrose."

"Primrose's grandmother comes from Jamaica." Vivica informed them. "And Su Lin's mum is from Vietnam."

"Hi," Su Lin said.

Vivica's a bit— Amelia began.

Shh. Poppy put a finger to her lips in case the others could tap into their messages.

"Hello, I'm Barbara." The remaining apprentice witch greeted them.

"Barbara is the seventh daughter of a seventh daughter and *very* special," Vivica said sarcastically.

"No more special than anyone else here," Barbara said quickly.

"Exactly right," Miss Hyacinth intervened. "Each of us has her own particular powers. Some of you will be natural fliers—" Poppy dug Amelia in the ribs "—and others will need more practice. But I promise you, girls, by the end of the night, you will all be flying perfectly. Now remember, each of your brooms has its own unique personality and must be treated accordingly, but certain basic rules apply to all. The first thing we will be doing tonight is to greet your brooms." Amelia pulled a face which Poppy ignored. "Are you ready, class?"

"Hello, brooms," they chorused.

"Very good. Now we will teach our brooms to hover."

Done this, Poppy thought, gaining a slight frown from the teacher and a glare from Amelia.

"Stretch out your hand, palm down, and give the command 'Hover'."

The girls did as they were told and six brooms floated horizontally in front of their owners.

"Mount your brooms."

"It's like getting on a horse," Vivica said.

I don't like horses. Amelia chewed her bottom lip.

Don't let her get to you, Poppy messaged.

I won't, Amelia messaged back and climbed on to her broom.

As soon as they were ready, Miss Hyacinth gave the command and the girls, led by Vivica, began to fly in a circle. Round and round they went, slowly at first, then faster and faster until Miss Hyacinth said, "Tell your brooms to stop and land."

"That was all right," Amelia said in surprise as

she stepped off her broom onto the wet grass.

"All you needed was a bit of confidence." Miss Hyacinth smiled at her. "It's hard at first, especially if you don't come from a family of witches. You've done really well, Amelia. So well, in fact, that you are ready for the next stage."

Poppy glanced at Amelia, expecting her to look worried but she was nodding enthusiastically.

The group divided into pairs and Miss Hyacinth pointed to an oak tree some distance away and told them they were to fly around it and back again. "Poppy and Amelia will go first, followed by Vivica and Primrose, then Su Lin and Barbara."

Barbara grinned at Su Lin and they did a high five. Primrose didn't look pleased that she'd been partnered with Vivica but Poppy was relieved that she and Amelia were going together.

"Remember to tell your brooms what you want them to do and where you want them to go. Do it politely and respectfully. That way they will look after you and you will look after them. First pair … one, two, three, fly!" Miss Hyacinth waved her hand and Poppy and Amelia were off.

Poppy went first. Knowing Amelia was not as keen on flying as she was she began by keeping her broom at a steady pace, but as she rose higher and Miss Hyacinth and the other girls dwindled into tiny figures far below she leaned forward and whispered, "Faster."

The broom accelerated, circling the tree at a speed that snatched Poppy's breath from her lungs, then turning and racing back to the starting point.

Miss Hyacinth waved them down but Poppy was enjoying herself too much to stop. Her broom seemed to be feeling the same way. As soon as she said "Go" it shot up into the night sky. It corkscrewed. It flew upside down. It looped the loop. Poppy held on shrieking with excitement. Until, *Poppy Barrington, it's time to land,* a warning voice came into her mind and she brought her broom to a perfect halt at Miss Hyacinth's feet.

"That was awesome," Poppy cried.

"The most awesome thing ever!" To Poppy's amazement Amelia was as excited as she was.

"Well." Miss Hyacinth frowned. Poppy went hot, then cold, and almost wished she'd obeyed the teacher's instructions.

It wouldn't have been so much fun, Amelia messaged.

We wouldn't be in trouble, Poppy replied.

"Hmm," Miss Hyacinth pursed her lips then her face relaxed and she smiled. "That was excellent flying. Poppy Barrington and Amelia Reeves, you have passed Level Four."

"Wow!" Poppy breathed.

"Yes!" Amelia shrieked.

"It's well deserved. You will be presented with your certificates when everyone else has done their test."

Vivica and Primrose were next. Vivica sat straight-backed as if riding a horse, Primrose was more relaxed. Then it was Su Lin and Barbara, who rode side by side and were laughing as they landed. After their first circuit the rest of the group put their brooms through their paces just as Poppy and Amelia had done. Then they waited, broomsticks in hand, to be told that they too had passed Level Four.

"That makes it perfect," Barbara said happily. "Doesn't it?" She looked at Vivica, who swallowed hard as if she had something stuck in her throat.

"Yes. I'm glad we all did well," Vivica said.

She's not as bad as I thought, Poppy messaged. Amelia, who was still wary of communicating while there were other witches about, grinned and nodded.

"Time for the presentations," Miss Hyacinth announced. They lined up and one by one she handed them their certificates.

"This is the best thing ever," Poppy said as she read the black letters on a purple background with a sprinkling of silver stars.

This is to certify that
Poppy Barrington
Has passed her Level Four flying test
With Distinction
Signed, Emer Hyacinth
Owner and teacher in charge of the Flying
Broomstick Academy

"I'm so happy!" Certificate in one hand, broomstick in the other, Poppy flung her arms into the air.

"I'm so tired. And happy too. Flying is the best thing. Now we know how to do it." Amelia stroked her broomstick and it rustled happily. "Let's go home. It'll be morning soon."

"Not already? I want to fly some more."

"You can't. Everyone else is leaving," Amelia pointed out. "Race you." She jumped on her broom and rose into the air.

"That's not fair," Poppy yelled and with a quick wave to the other girls she flew after her.

They whizzed over The Downs, shot down the hill and along the river. Poppy had almost caught up with Amelia when she saw Bubbles Mike, her dad's best friend. Poppy knew she shouldn't, but she had to do it. Swooping overhead, she waved and called out leaving him staring at her in amazement as she flew past.

Amelia was still in front, but by the time they turned into Coronation Road Poppy was gaining on her. Urged on by their riders both brooms put on a spurt. Neck to neck they flew until they landed at Poppy's door.

"I won," Poppy said.

"You did not."

"My foot touched the ground before yours."

"It didn't."

"It did."

"It was a draw," Amelia said.

"Suppose so," Poppy admitted. "See you tomorrow."

"You mean today." Amelia gave an enormous yawn. "That was fun but why do witch things always happen…"

"In the witching hour," they said together.

Poppy watched Amelia go down the road, took her house key out of her pocket then put it back again. It was still dark. There was still time.

"Please broom, let's go flying."

The broom rustled its twigs. Poppy got on and they flew over the houses, above the roofs, round church spires, along the river, under the Suspension Bridge, over the Suspension Bridge, and finally, as the sky was turning pink, they flew home.

Chapter 12

MUM'S ALARM WAS ringing when Poppy crept up the stairs, changed into her school uniform, went back downstairs and into the kitchen to prepare Mia's garlic paste sandwiches. She wasn't tired, she told herself. Her eyes didn't itch. Her mouth wasn't dry. Her skin didn't feel as if ants were crawling all over it. Poppy rubbed her arm over her face, drank some water, and smeared a smidgeon of paste on a slice of bread.

"That's yuk." Jake came into the room trailing his blanket behind him.

"So? You don't have to eat it." *It's for a real live vampire who'd suck all the blood out of your body if I asked her to.* Poppy dropped the knife. *I didn't mean that,* she thought horrified.

"It's gone on the floor," Jake pointed out.

"I can see that." Poppy scowled at her brother.

"Bernard's going to lick it." Was Jake being deliberately annoying? "I'll pick it up," he offered.

"Oh leave it. Bernard go away."

The dachshund cocked his head on one side and looked at her.

"Basket," Poppy snarled.

"Poppy?" Mum came in. "Were you shouting

at the dog?"

"Sorry," Poppy muttered.

"She was letting him lick the knife."

"You know you mustn't do that," Mum chided.

"Mmm," Poppy grunted. Mum was right. Jake was right. So why were they making her so angry?

"Are you okay?" Mum filled the kettle. "You look tired."

"I'm not," Poppy snapped. "I'm fine."

I can't help it if everyone's being so annoying.

"If you're not feeling well you don't have to go to school. I can work from home today."

"I don't want to stay home." *It's my turn to make Mia's sandwiches. Though I don't see why she has to have them every day.*

"Well, if you're sure have some breakfast first and then we can see—"

"I told you, I'm okay," Poppy interrupted. *Except I'm not. I don't mean to be cross, but I can't seem to help it.*

Bernard pressed himself against her leg as if to say he didn't mind being shouted at and she was still the best. Instead of petting him Poppy pushed him away. The dog hung his head and whimpered sadly.

"Poppy's being mean to Bernard," Jake said.

I don't like this, Poppy thought. *It's not me. I'm not horrid to everyone … except when Mum says I'm overtired. Perhaps she's right and I should stay home.* She told Mum she'd changed her mind and messaged Amelia asking her to make a garlic-paste sandwich for Mia, then went upstairs, put on her pyjamas and crawled back into bed.

Pulling the duvet around her ears she yawned a couple of times, shut her eyes and tried to relax; but her brain was still fizzing and whirling with the excitement of flying. She saw herself racing towards the Suspension Bridge. Lit up, the bridge was like a golden chain flung across the darkness of the gorge. Up and over she flew. Down and under she dived. Upside down, the right way up, looping the loop, laughing and shrieking with exhilaration.

More awake than ever, Poppy took a book from the shelf, propped herself up on the pillows and tried to lose herself in the story. It was no good; all she could think about was getting her flying certificate from Miss Hyacinth.

Poppy gave up the idea of reading and snuggled down again. She lay on her back. She lay on her side. She lay with her legs straight. She curled her knees up to her chin. Whatever position she tried she could not get to sleep.

Halfway through the morning she went downstairs to lie on the sofa and watch the most boring film she could find. That didn't work either. Poppy had enough. She was bored and fed up and she wanted to see her friends.

"I'm feeling better. Can I go back to school this afternoon?" she asked.

"If you really want to," Mum said.

"I do," Poppy said brightly.

"Then I guess you're well enough." Mum smiled.

WHEN POPPY ARRIVED at school it was almost the end of the lunch break. She registered at the office before going out into the yard where Amelia and Mia were standing together talking in low voices. Neither of them looked up as Poppy strode towards them.

"It was awesome," Amelia was saying. "I'm not scared of flying anymore."

"That's cool. Oh hi, Poppy. Amelia said you weren't coming in."

"I changed my mind."

"I was just telling Mia about—"

"Hmm," Poppy grunted.

Amelia and Mia looked at her in amazement.

"What's wrong?" Mia asked.

"Nothing." Poppy shrugged. *You've only taken my best friend off me that's all.*

"I don't mean it," she said out loud.

"What?" Amelia said.

"I don't know." Poppy sighed. "I feel strange and kind of… Hey come on, that's the bell and it's

French and I hate French. Madame Prunella's okay but I can't ever get it right. My tongue won't twist round the words. Why can't everyone speak the same?"

"Cos, that would be strange," Amelia said.

"Well I think … if we had a sp—"

"Poppy, shut up," Amelia said.

"It's like you've turned the word tap on and you can't turn it off," Mia said.

"That's really funny." Amelia giggled.

"*I* don't think so," Poppy said with a toss of the head. *They're getting at me again. Except it is funny but somehow I can't laugh about it. Maybe Mum was right and I am ill. But I don't feel as if I am. I just feel … kind of wriggly.*

In French, she couldn't keep still and was sent out of the room. In English, she couldn't keep quiet and was given lines. In History, which was her favourite subject, she tried so hard to behave that she didn't dare move or speak.

"I think the magic's done something to you," Mia said while they were walking home.

"No it hasn't," Poppy protested.

"She might have a spell on her," Amelia suggested.

"Who put it on? Unless it was you," Poppy snapped.

"Course it wasn't me. Why would I want to make you so cross all the time?"

"Could it have been someone else?" Mia asked.

Poppy shook her head then slapped her forehead as she realised what she had done. "It was me," she confessed.

"You?" Amelia and Mia spoke together.

"I was worried that I wouldn't wake up in time for the flying lesson so I cast a staying-awake spell."

"That's it!" Amelia cried. "All you've got to do is take it off. I can do it for you. I'm getting good at spells – I've been practising. Come to my house and I'll do it."

Poppy was not sure that the spell she'd put on herself could be removed by someone else but the other two were so keen that she agreed to let Amelia try.

Up in Amelia's bedroom the three girls sat on the floor and held hands. In the middle of their circle Amelia put a cup of water and a candle. Watching the flame flickering on the surface of the water made Poppy feel drowsy, but Amelia told her that she had to say the magic words for the spell to work.

"Are you sure it'll be okay?" Mia looked worried.

"Nothing is going to go wrong," Amelia assured her.

"We know what we're doing," Poppy added.

Amelia began to chant the sleeping spell and Poppy's eyes grew heavy, her head drooped, her grip loosened and she fell backwards onto the carpet.

"Oh!" Amelia said. "It wasn't meant to work straightaway."

"So what do we do?" Mia looked at the sleeping Poppy.

"We wake her up and she can go home to bed and everything will be okay. Poppy—" Amelia clapped her hands "—get up. You can't sleep on my floor."

Poppy's eyelids fluttered but instead of opening her eyes she snored and turned over on her side.

"She's not waking up. What can we do?" Amelia said.

"This." Mia tipped the cup of water over Poppy's head. Poppy snuffled but didn't wake. Amelia shouted in her ear. Mia opened the window to let the cold air in. They shrieked and banged and yelled. Poppy slept on.

"There's got to be a waking-up spell." Amelia turned to her handbook.

"Or an antidote," Mia said.

"There's nothing in here." Amelia was frantically riffling through the pages.

"Don't worry, the spell will wear off," her handbook said soothingly.

"But when?" Mia was too worried to be surprised by a talking book.

"When the spell comes to an end."

"When will that happen? Tomorrow? Or in a

hundred years' time?" Amelia asked.

"Mmm," said the book. "You are not experienced enough to do anything that lasts as long as that. So I should say—" it fluttered its pages "—she should be awake by tomorrow evening."

"Tomorrow!" Amelia and Mia chorused.

"What can we do till then?" Amelia asked. The book was silent. Amelia looked at Mia.

Mia shrugged then said, "Can you fly her home on your broomstick?"

"I can try." Amelia picked up her broom and told it to hover. It did as it was asked and hung suspended in the air as Amelia took Poppy's shoulders, Mia grabbed Poppy's feet, and together they heaved her up and balanced her, head down, over the broom. As soon as Poppy was on board the broom wobbled, dipped, and sank until it was almost touching the ground.

"It's no good," Amelia said. "Land," she told the broom.

"No," Mia cried. "Poppy will fall on top of it. We've got to get her off first. You stand behind her and keep her steady." Mia pushed Poppy to her feet while Amelia held her upright and the broom flew off and propped itself in its corner. Then the two girls lowered Poppy back onto the bedside rug.

"We can't leave her here. Dad will see her … and what will I say?"

"You can't tell him the truth, can you? I suppose that's the problem if you have parents who aren't magic like you."

"I wasn't magic until Mr Harrison came to teach us. Sometimes I wish—" Amelia glanced at the book and the broomstick and changed her mind. Magic might cause problems but it opened up a whole new world to explore. And it meant she could fly. "If I tried to explain, Dad would never believe me. He'd think Poppy was ill and when she wouldn't wake up he'd call an ambulance."

"I've never been in an ambulance and I don't suppose I ever will. Vampires don't get sick the same way people do."

"That's not helping," Amelia complained.

"It's all right," Mia said. "I've got a plan but we have to wait till Chris and Hera are awake."

"It's dark already." Amelia pulled open the curtains. A large yellow moon hung over the roof tops and the sky was sprinkled with stars.

"Then I'll text them and we can get on with the first bit while we wait for them to arrive. Is there anything in that book that would make me look and sound like Poppy?"

"A glamour. That's what you require. You'll find it on page forty-four. However, it takes some skill but—" the book said.

"We only need it for a few minutes."

"Very well." The book obligingly opened itself

at the right page.

"Are they here yet?" Amelia asked before she started casting the spell.

Mia glanced at the window. "They're outside. Those two bats are Chris and Hera."

Amelia began to chant. Minutes later there were two girls that looked like Poppy in her bedroom. One was sound asleep on the rug, the other was standing beside her.

Amelia invited the vampires to enter and the bats flew in and transformed themselves into Mia's parents.

"We've got to hurry. The glamour won't last long." Amelia took Poppy's keys and a large handful of forgetting powder from her friend's pocket. Leaving the real Poppy asleep on the floor, she and the Poppy-who-was-Mia hurried down the stairs.

"I hope this works," Amelia said when they reached Poppy's house.

"Course it will. Poppy's mum and dad will think she's home. Then Chris and Hera will bring the real Poppy back. Anyway, if it doesn't work you've got the forgetting powder."

Using Poppy's key, Amelia opened the front door.

"Mum," Poppy-who-was-Mia called. "It's just me and Amelia. We're going up to my room."

"Fine. Did you have a good time?"

"Yeth, thanths." Mia lisped as the glamour

faded and her teeth sharpened. The two girls raced up the stairs, but before they reached the top, Mia was already changing back. By the time they reached the bedroom she had Poppy's face and glasses and her own vampire teeth and plaits. Amelia stood with her back to the door to keep everyone out as the last of the spell drained away. Mia's face wavered like a reflection in a pool and then settled into itself.

"That's better. It was horrible having human teeth."

A low growling sound came from the other side of the door.

"It's Bernard. He knows something's wrong," Amelia said.

The growling grew louder and was followed by a bark.

"Poppy," Jake ran down the corridor. "Me and Bernard want to come into your room."

"You can't," Amelia said. "We're doing something." She gestured to Mia to take her place at the door, then ran across the room and opened the window.

"Please enter."

She stood aside and Hera, followed by Chris with Poppy in his arms, flew in.

"It's not fair." Jake banged on the door.

"What do we do?" Mia asked.

"Mum!" Jake wailed.

Chris lay Poppy gently on the bed.

"Poppy." Mrs Barrington's voice floated up the stairs. It had that edge to it that meant she was coming to see what was going on.

"Time to make an exit," Hera said and before Amelia could thank them the three vampires were gone.

Bernard barked and scrabbled frantically at the door. Jake opened it and he and Bernard burst in. The dog raced to the window. He jumped up and down barking frantically.

"Shh," Amelia cried. "Please, shush."

She slammed the window shut and pulled down the blind. Taking a pinch of forgetting powder she sprinkled it on Bernard's nose.

The dog gave a yip, looked around, then trotted out of the bedroom.

"Why is Poppy asleep?" Jake wandered over to the bed and was poking his sister to wake her up.

"Cos she's tired. And so are you. I'll take you back to your room." Amelia held out her hand.

"I'm not sleepy."

"Course you're not," Amelia agreed. "Here, you've got something on your pyjama top." As she bent to brush off the non-existent speck she threw a pinch of forgetting powder into the air.

"Bye Poppy," she called loudly as she took Jake back to bed. "I'm going, Mrs Barrington," she added as she ran down the stairs. "I can see myself out."

She opened the front door and before she

closed it, threw some of the powder over her shoulder. Out in the street she let out her breath.

Doing magic could be very complicated. One spell could lead to another, and then another. Poppy's staying-awake spell had led to the sleeping spell, then to the waking-up one and then the glamour, and finally she had to use the forgetting powder. It was enough to make Amelia's head spin but at least this time they had got away with it.

Chapter 13

POPPY WOKE UP the next day still wearing her school uniform. *How did that happen?* she thought, kicking off her shoes. *Did I fall asleep when I came home? Why didn't Mum wake me?*

She sat up, rubbed her eyes and her stomach gurgled loudly. Jumping out of bed, Poppy quickly brushed her teeth, splashed some water on her face and ran downstairs to the kitchen where Mum was making toast and Dad and Jake were eating cereal.

"I'm starving," Poppy said. "Did we have tea last night?"

"Of course we did and you…" Mum shook her head. "You were at Amelia's and I can't remember what time you came in."

You sound like you've got a forgetting spell on you, Poppy thought as she helped herself to a large bowl of cereal. *I didn't put it on you so what's going on?* She ate another bowlful then started making Mia's sandwiches.

"You're not still hungry, are you?" Mum said.

"A bit." Poppy held her breath as she spread garlic paste over the bread. "I might want something at break."

"There's chocolate in the cupboard."

Poppy's knife stopped in mid-paste. She loved chocolate and hated garlic but she had to refuse. Mia's treatment was going well. She no longer turned paler than pale each time she took a bite and sometimes she managed a whole sandwich. Maybe one day soon she'd be ready to try a cheese and onion crisp.

"I'm all right," Poppy said, wrapping the sandwich in as many layers of kitchen paper as she could to stop the smell of garlic spreading through her bag.

AT BREAK TIME Poppy, Amelia and Mia went to their usual place in the yard. It was a shaded corner away from the rest of the school, and because it was damp and dreary no one else ever went there.

"Your dad flew me home?" Poppy said after the others told her what had happened.

"We didn't know what else to do," Mia said.

"I suppose it is useful having a vampire as a friend." Poppy grinned.

"Shh." Amelia elbowed her as a group of Year Seven boys came running after a football. "They could have heard you."

"But they didn't. In any case—" Poppy patted her pocket "—ever since those dogs I always carry some forgetting powder around with me."

"Not enough for a whole class. Or a whole school," Amelia said.

"No one must ever find out what I am," Mia said.

"Is that what happened in the other schools you went to?" Amelia asked.

"Not exactly, but people started saying how different I was, how my mum never stayed around in the playground like the other mums and how she never asked anyone back to our house and I couldn't go on playdates because I couldn't eat human food."

"You can a bit. You ate a whole sandwich this morning," Poppy said.

"It looks like our idea is working. Do you want to try one of these?" Amelia took out a packet of cheese and onion crisps.

"Oh!" The faintest flush came into Mia's cheeks. "I think I might."

Amelia ripped open the packet and offered it to Mia.

"Only if you're sure," Poppy said quickly.

"I'm sure." Mia gave them a quick smile revealing a brief flash of sharp white fangs, then very, very cautiously she reached out and took a crisp. Holding it between finger and thumb she lifted it to her lips. Halfway up she stopped, shut

her eyes, and took a deep breath. "It smells …
delicious."

Go on, Poppy thought. *Eat it.*

Mia opened her mouth; she licked out her
tongue. "Oh!" she cried.

Poppy looked at Amelia. Amelia looked at
Poppy.

Crunch. Mia's mouth closed around the crisp.

They waited.

"That was the best thing – ever," Mia said.

"You did it!" Amelia cried.

"We did it," Poppy said.

"Yes we did, all three of us." Amelia turned to
Mia and they gave each other high fives.

"Does that mean you can eat like us?" Amelia
asked as they walked back to class.

"Not yet," Poppy said. "We have to do it
slowly. Like babies."

"Babies?" Mia said.

"They start off with milk and go on to proper
food, bit by bit."

"That's because they don't have teeth," Amelia
said.

Without meaning to they both looked at Mia.

"Some of my teeth look like yours and I could
crunch the crisps really easily. But I've been
thinking … I don't know if I really want to be—"

"Like us?" Poppy asked.

"I can't be like you. I'm not a witch. No, I meant
I don't know if I want to be much more of a

human."

"Because of your mum and dad?"

Mia nodded.

"It's what they want for you. They said so." Amelia was puzzled.

"I know, but if I'm different from them one day I'll grow up and be old and they won't … and I couldn't bear it when—"

Mia looked so sad that Poppy gave her a hug.

"It's all right for you," Mia said with a sob.

"No it isn't," Amelia said. "We're different from our families too … and sometimes it's hard."

"And sometimes it's fun," Poppy said quickly. They were almost in the classroom and she didn't want them to arrive looking as if something really terrible had happened. "Look—" she pointed to the poster on the wall "—it's the Halloween Disco on Friday."

"We've got to go to that," Amelia said.

"We'll all dress up … as…"

"Witches?" Amelia asked.

"Vampires!" Poppy grinned.

IT WAS THE day of the disco and Amelia and Mia arranged to meet at Poppy's house. Amelia arrived first.

"Why are you two sitting on the stairs?" Jake asked.

"We're waiting," his sister replied.

"For Trick or Treat?"

"Maybe."

At that moment the doorbell rang. Bernard pattered down the hall and barked while Jake jumped up to reach the latch. He was taking so long that Poppy pushed past him and scooped up the dog. Bernard squirmed and yapped making it very difficult for her to open the door.

"It's a vampire!" Jake stared at the girl on the threshold. Dressed in black with dark hair and bright red lips, she held two carrier bags.

"It's Mia. Come in." Poppy stepped aside. Bernard took one look at Mia, wrenched himself out of Poppy's grasp, and raced off to the kitchen to hide in his basket.

"He doesn't like me," Mia said sadly.

"You scared him," Jake said. "Cos you're a vampire."

"We're all going to be vampires," Poppy said hastily. "We're going upstairs to get changed and you can't come with us."

Mia brought black cloaks and dresses. Poppy's mum had given them some lipstick, and they had bought plastic fangs to complete the look.

"I'll take a picture," Amelia said, when they were ready.

"Not of me."

"Why not, Mia? You look great." Poppy linked her arm and flashed her fangs. "Go on Amelia show her."

Amelia looked at the screen, frowned and handed her phone to Poppy. "It's a good one of you but Mia's not there."

"That's weird," Poppy said.

"No it's not. It's like mirrors. We vampires can't be seen cos we don't have reflections."

"That's grim," Amelia exclaimed.

"Not really. It means I don't have to worry about what I look like."

"Will you start to appear if you get more human?" Poppy was beginning to understand why Mia didn't want to get rid of all her vampire traits. How strange it would be if she was the only one in her house that could see her reflection, or take a selfie. "You'd be like a ghost in a mirror."

"Ghosts are all right. Granny and Grandpa can be fun."

"We could have asked them to come to the disco with us," Amelia said.

"No way! They'd only cause trouble and I want to go with my friends. Just the three of us." Mia smiled shyly and a warm feeling spread from Poppy's toes to the top of her head.

Chapter 14

"THE THREE OF you look amazing," Mum said, when they trooped downstairs in their vampire costumes.

"Very realistic," Dad added. "If I met you in the street I'd cross to the other side – because you know what they say about vampires." The three girls looked at him expectantly. "The first bite is the worst."

"Dad!" Poppy groaned.

"You're scary." Jake clutched his blanket.

"No we're not. We're only us. See." Amelia pulled the plastic fangs out of her mouth.

"Now you." Jake pointed to Mia.

"No time," Poppy said. "We've got to go, or we'll be late."

At the gate they turned and waved. Jake waved back, his blanket a bright flag in the glow of the streetlights.

"That was close," Poppy said.

"Your dad said we looked so real." Amelia giggled.

"We do." Mia bared her fangs and lunged at Poppy's neck. "Argh!" she growled.

"Argh!" Poppy growled back.

A group of little kids coming back with their mums from Trick or Treating stopped and stared. One girl started to cry.

"It's all right," Poppy called. "We won't bite."

"Though it is time you were home." Mia sounded so serious that a shiver travelled up Poppy's spine. "Ghosts and phantoms will be out later," Mia explained after the mums had hurried their children away. "On Halloween they get up to all sorts of things and some of them are really mean and scary."

THEY HEARD THE disco as soon as they walked through the school gates. It was Year Seven's turn to decorate Ashley Park School for Halloween and greenish light glowed in classroom windows illuminating flights of paper bats, crescent moons, and witches on broomsticks. A pair of pumpkins grinned evilly on either side of the main door and the foyer was full of Year Seven pupils. Dressed as skeletons, witches, zombies and ghosts, they were queuing to hand in their tickets to Mr Charles, 7C's form tutor, who sat at the desk with Madame Prunella. He was dressed as a wizard and she was a witch.

"I wonder if Mr Harrison is here," Amelia

whispered.

"His mum won't let him out. You know what he was like with magic," Poppy whispered back.

"I wonder if he misses it?" Amelia said.

Poppy did not reply as they reached the head of the queue.

"Poppy, Mia, Amelia … my, you look very…" Madame Prunella hesitated.

"Real." Mia grinned.

She's enjoying herself, Poppy thought.

She's loving being herself, Amelia messaged.

Disco lights flashed and music blared as they walked into the hall.

"Vampires. Cool." Will was standing with a group of friends. The boys were dressed as skeletons, zombies and wizards.

"You're the best," another lad said. "The others look dressed up. You look—"

"Real," Poppy, Amelia and Mia chorused.

"He said we were the best," Mia sighed happily as they went off to dance.

"That's cos we are," Poppy shouted above the music. And they danced and danced.

Will and his friends joined them during the break for refreshments. They helped themselves from plates stacked high with spider biscuits, eerie eyeball pops, kiwi slime pies, pastry snakes, zombie fingers, and bat cookies. There were also bowls of crisps, plain ones, barbeque flavour and—

"Cheese and onion!" Mia breathed.

The drink was juice, red as blood. Mia held a cupful to her lips but Poppy was almost certain she didn't drink any.

Then it was time for Halloween games and everyone wanted Poppy, Amelia and Mia in their teams. The first game was bobbing for apples. Mia, who was not used to being chosen for a team, waited at the back.

Poppy managed two apples for her team, Amelia one for hers. Then it was Mia's turn. She took a breath, ducked her head in the water and aimed for the apple bobbing closest to the edge. She closed her teeth around it.

"One!" her team called. Down she went again. "Two! Three! Four!" they counted and when the whistle blew for the end of the game Mia's team had won.

Next it was "Pin the Tail on the Witch's Cat" and Poppy and Amelia watched as Mia attached the tail in exactly the right place. *Bet she can see through the blindfold,* Poppy messaged.

Wish she was on our team, Amelia messaged back.

With every game they played, being a vampire gave Mia an advantage. Poppy and Amelia didn't mind. They were glad to see her joining in with the rest of the class and they whooped and cheered with all the others when her team won. She even received the most votes for the best dancer.

"I'm having the best time ever and I want it to go on all night," Mia said once the competition was over.

Me too. Then I'll get on my broom and fly to the stars, Poppy messaged.

Amelia shook her head and yawned.

Mr Charles climbed onto the stage, held up his hand and the music stopped, the mirror ball spun to a halt, and the hall lights were switched on.

"Time to go home, Year Seven," Mr Charles said. "Your parents and guardians will be waiting to collect you and Mr Jones, the caretaker, is ready to lock up for the night. Goodnight and see you all on Monday."

Everyone began to leave, laughing and talking as they made for the exit. The night was chill with frost and no one waited around. Very soon the schoolyard was empty except for three vampire girls standing at the gates.

"Where's Dad?" Poppy's breath spiralled into the air. "He's supposed to be picking us up but I can't see his car." She peered down the street.

"I'm cold." Amelia rubbed her arms. "Shall we start walking?"

"Certainly not." Mr Charles appeared behind them. "That wouldn't be safe. I'm sure your dad will be here in a minute. Poppy, do you have your phone?" She nodded. "Then why don't you give him a call? In the meantime come back inside and

I'll wait with you."

"No, sir. We'll be okay," Amelia said.

Mr Charles looked doubtful. "I can't leave students out here alone while I'm on duty and it's very cold."

"Then we'll wait by the front door. Dad's on his way." Poppy put her phone back in her pocket. "He was watching the football and he forgot the time. He says he's very sorry but he'll be here in a minute."

"Mr Jones is still inside. He can keep an eye on us if you're worried," Amelia said.

"If you're sure." Mr Charles's teeth were chattering.

"Yes," Poppy said. "There he is, I can see the headlights."

"In that case have a good weekend."

"We will," they chorused as he hurried off to the teachers' carpark at the back of the building.

"Where is your dad?" Amelia was looking down the road.

"At the garage." Poppy raised her eyebrows. "He really is on his way, now that he's got enough petrol to get here."

"He better be here soon. I'm freezing," Amelia complained.

"You should have brought a coat. That's what Mum always says," Poppy teased. Amelia didn't smile and because Poppy was feeling guilty, as it was her dad who was keeping them out in the cold, she said, "You and Mia go and wait inside. I'll come and get you when he turns up."

"We're not leaving you on your own," Mia said. "Let's go over there. It's out of the wind and we'll still be able to see your dad's car."

The three of them hurried away to a corner by the bins and found a sheltered spot. After the fun and excitement of the evening none of them had much to say. Amelia wrapped her arms around herself and thought about her warm bed. Poppy wondered what it would be like to go flying on Halloween, and Mia stared out across the yard thinking how brilliant the disco had been.

Two figures scuttling out of the shadows caught her attention. Dressed in black with baseball caps pulled low over their faces they headed for a side door.

"Look," she whispered as the caretaker let them in.

"That's not right," Poppy said. "Shall we go and see what they're doing?"

"We can't. Your dad's here," Amelia said as a car swept in through the gates.

"Sorry I'm late. Jump in and I'll get you home in no time." Mr Barrington leaned across and opened the passenger door.

"Thanks for picking us up." Amelia clambered into the back seat.

"No problem." As Poppy's dad turned to speak to her, Amelia muttered a few words under her breath. Mr Barrington gave a great yawn, his eyes closed, his head dropped forward and —

"He's asleep," Mia said.

"I did the sleeping spell."

"You know what happened last time." Mia looked at Poppy.

"I did a short one. At least I think I did. So it should only last for a bit."

"Long enough for us to go and see what's happening?"

Amelia nodded and she and Mia looked at Poppy.

"Okay. I'm up for it." She set off towards the school building. "What are you two waiting for?"

Chapter 15

THE MAIN DOOR to the school was still open but as they stepped inside it shut behind them and everything went dark – except for a small light above the keypad.

"They've probably locked the doors and set the alarm. How are we going to get out?" Poppy asked.

"We'll…" Amelia shrugged.

"Ask Mr Jones?" Poppy said sarcastically.

"We won't have to," Mia said as the light flickered then died. "Looks like it's been switched off. Shh. I can hear something."

"I can't see anything." Poppy blinked.

"It's all right," Mia said. "I can see in the dark. Besides it's never really dark in cities so your eyes will soon get used to it."

"What do you think they're doing?" Amelia whispered.

"I'm not sure, but if we go to Jonesy's office, we'll find out." Mia led the way along deserted corridors that stretched into pools of darkness, past locked classrooms and round to the back of the hall. The air here was warmer and there was a faint hum from the boiler.

The door to the caretaker's room was slightly ajar and by keeping close to the wall they could see and hear what was going on inside. Mr Jones sat at the table with the two men he had let into the building.

That's Jonesy's grandson, Kyle, Amelia messaged. "I know who he is," she mouthed to Mia, knowing that the vampire girl would be able to see her lips in the dark.

"The van's round the back and me and Nathan are all ready to go." Kyle took a gulp of coffee.

"Are you sure the alarm's off?" Nathan asked.

"I told you, it's done," Mr Jones snapped.

"Then we'll be getting on with it." Nathan pushed back his chair.

"Hold your horses," Mr Jones said. "We've got all night."

"You have, Granddad, but Ted's waiting for the goods and if we don't get them to him as per arrangement he's not going to be happy." Kyle stood up. "It's okay, you don't have to come with us. We know our way to the IT rooms, don't we Nath?"

"That was the only lesson I ever liked in this stinking hole," Nathan replied. "Come on mate."

Poppy and Amelia flattened themselves against the wall and the two men came out of the room. The girls waited until they'd walked down the corridor then, *We've got to do something,* Poppy messaged frantically.

Call the police, Amelia messaged back.

Can't. My phone's gone dead.

It's okay, I've got mine. The pocket of Amelia's dress was not very deep and as she put her hand inside, she knocked her phone to the ground.

"What's that? Who's there?" Mr Jones jumped up from his chair.

"Run!" Poppy cried but instead of doing as she said Amelia bent down to pick up her phone, giving Mr Jones the chance to grab her arm and twist it behind her back.

"Got you," he snarled.

"Leave her alone." Poppy kept out of the caretaker's reach. "If you don't I'll call the police."

Mr Jones laughed. "I'm the one that's calling the police. Pupils lurking on school premises after hours. Up to no good, that's what you are." Still holding Amelia he edged her towards the storeroom, unlocked the door and shoved her inside. "There's one of you. Now for the other one." He lunged at Poppy who took off as fast as she could and banged straight into Kyle.

"No you don't." Holding her so tightly she could hardly breathe, Kyle pushed Poppy in beside Amelia and locked the door. They heard him say, "Sorry about this, Granddad." Then there was a thump and the sound of a body falling to the ground.

"Kyle's hit Jonesy." Amelia clutched hold of Poppy.

"That's so he can say he's had nothing to do with the break in, or locking us up. We've got to get out and stop them robbing the school."

"I'll try the window." Amelia blundered her way past cardboard boxes full of paper towels and toilet rolls. "The catch is stiff, but it's going to—" she pushed, then pushed again "—open," she said triumphantly as a blast of freezing air blew into the room.

They scrambled out of the window and raced across to the carpark.

"Dad, wake up!" Poppy yelled. Mr Barrington's eyelids fluttered, then his mouth fell open and he snored loudly. Poppy pulled at the car door, which did not open. "It's no good. We can't get in."

"Where's Mia?" Amelia looked at Poppy.

"I don't know – she sort of disappeared."

"Well, she'll have a phone."

"Maybe she ran after Kyle and his mate. They were going to the IT rooms. That's where she'll be."

They skirted around the outside of the school till they came to the IT rooms. A white van was parked outside the door and lights were moving inside one of the classrooms. Crouching low, they peeped in through the window. Kyle and Nathan were stuffing laptops and tablets into sports bags.

"Get a move on," Kyle said. "We've got to get going before Granddad comes round and calls the police."

"He knows what to tell them?"

"Course he does. He got hit on the head by burglars. The break-in's got nothing to do with him."

"What about those girls?"

"He'll think of something. Smart man, my granddad."

They don't know about Mia, Poppy messaged.

Where is she? Amelia messaged back.

I don't know. I can't see her.

She can't have … she wouldn't have … run away? Even considering the idea made Poppy feel bad but what other explanation was there for their missing friend?

Maybe she's gone for help, Amelia messaged.

Then where are the police?

"That's the lot. Nothing else worth nicking." Kyle zipped up the last of the bags. "I'll start loading these in the van."

They're going to get away, Poppy messaged.

And there's nothing we can do about it, Amelia added.

They stared glumly through the window. Kyle slung a bag over his shoulder, picked up two more, and made for the door.

"Put those down." Mia stepped out of the shadows. Her eyes glowed red, her lips were furled, revealing sharp white fangs.

"Get out of my way, or I'll—" Kyle was trying

to sound brave but his voice trembled.

"Or you'll what?" Mia smiled such a terrible smile that even though she was their friend Poppy felt a twinge of fear.

"She'll take a bite out of you." A small round ghost materialised.

"And drink some of your blood." A larger ghost with shaggy hair and a beard manifested beside her.

"You're not real." Kyle shook so much he dropped his bags.

"Of course they're not. They're kids playing tricks. It's Halloween, remember," his mate said.

"Tricks is it?"

"Halloween is it?" The two ghosts floated forward.

"Eek!" Nathan shrieked. "Go away. You can't hurt me. You're just halogens."

"I think he means hallucinations," Grandpa Ghost said. "Don't they teach you anything at school these days?"

"I've gone all cold." Kyle quavered. Wrapping his arms around himself, he backed away.

"Shows that you shouldn't mess with vampires." Mia stood in front of him. She spread out her arms and the cloak she was wearing gave her the shape of a bat. A bat which grew larger and larger as the two burglars cowered and whimpered with fear.

"And you certainly shouldn't tangle with

ghosts." Granny and Grandpa swirled and whirled around the terrified men as they stumbled blindly towards the door.

"Now!" Poppy cried and she and Amelia dashed forward. As Kyle and Nathan burst out of the room she stuck out her foot. Kyle tripped and sprawled on the floor. Nathan, who was right behind him, fell over his prone body. Amelia lifted her hand and whispered the sleeping spell. The burglars' eyes closed, their chests moved up and down and they slept.

"Mia, phone the police," Poppy said.

"What? Who? Why?" Mia looked completely bewildered.

"What's wrong with her?" Amelia asked.

"Oh don't worry. It takes them like that sometimes. It's the energy draining away. She'll be all right in a minute or two," Granny Ghost said. "Goodbye girls. We haven't had such fun on Halloween for centuries but we have to go now." And with a wave of their hands the ghosts disappeared.

"Oh, by the way—" the larger ghost was back "—we teleported the van's keys to the rubbish bin at the back of the school."

"Grandpa Ghost? What are you doing here? Whoops!" Mia swayed. "I feel a bit funny."

Amelia put her arm around Mia's waist and helped her sit down while Poppy used Mia's phone to ring the police.

They arrived with a screaming of sirens and flashing of blue lights to find Kyle and Nathan neatly tied up and sports bags full of the school's laptops and tablets beside them.

"You've done a great job," a policeman said as he handcuffed the two burglars.

"There's Mr Jones too. He was part of it." Poppy took one of the policemen to the caretaker's office where Mr Jones was lying on the floor groaning loudly.

"That's her. That's one of the kids that broke in." The caretaker heaved himself into a sitting position and pointed at Poppy.

"And stole the tablets? I don't think so. We've got your grandson for that," the policeman said.

"Well I never. Who would have thought that my Kyle was such a bad boy?" Mr Jones staggered to his feet. "Fancy hitting his old granddad over the head."

"You told him to." Poppy was determined that the caretaker was not going to get away with anything. "You let him into the school. We got locked in after the Halloween Disco and we were trying to get out when you grabbed us and shut us in the storeroom."

"I never did." Mr Jones tried his best to sound angry.

"We'll see about that," the policeman said. "In the meantime I'm taking you down to the police station with the other two. What about you girls, how are you getting home?"

"My dad…" Poppy trailed off not knowing if Amelia's spell was still working. "He'll be waiting in the carpark."

"If you're sure?"

"Yes. He said he'd be here and he's…" She was going to say *never late* even though that wasn't exactly true, but at that moment Mr Barrington came running towards them.

"Poppy, are you all right? Amelia said you were in here. I thought you were—"

"Yes Dad," Poppy said before he could remember that she'd been about to get in the car when he unexpectedly fell asleep. "Can we go home? I'm feeling really—" she yawned loudly "—tired."

As they crossed the yard, Poppy saw that Mia and Amelia were waiting by the car. Beside them were two ghosts. One tall and bearded, the other small and plump.

How am I going to explain them?

Poppy wished she had some forgetting powder in her pocket but Dad showed no signs of seeing anything unusual. He unlocked the car and told them to get in.

"Not you Mia," Grandpa Ghost said. "Come with us. It's Halloween. It's time to party."

"No thanks. I'm going with the others." Mia said.

"Don't be so stuffy. You're getting like your

mum and dad. They'll be sitting at home with a bottle of AB Neg and watching horror movies instead of spreading their wings and soaring with the rest of us."

"Granny!" Mia hissed.

"It's all part of this trying to be human business," Granny said sadly.

That's what you were once, Poppy wanted to say but didn't. Dad might not be able to hear or see the ghosts but that didn't mean he wouldn't hear her speaking to them.

"I knew no good would come of it," Grandpa Ghost said.

"You've got to accept what you are," Granny added.

"Can we go now, please Mr Barrington?" Mia climbed into the back of the car beside Amelia. Poppy sat at the front.

"I'll drop you off first, Mia. After all this excitement you'll be glad to be home."

"Yes," the vampire girl said firmly, waving goodbye to the two ghostly figures.

Chapter 16

THE BARRINGTON FAMILY were having breakfast the next morning when Mum's mobile rang. "It's a journalist from the *Evening Post*," she said. "She wants to do an interview with Poppy about the burglary. They're going to do a feature on it."

"Brave Schoolgirls Foil Thieves!" Dad declared.

"Wow!" said Poppy. "That's amazing."

"I thought you'd agree." Mum sorted out the details while Poppy mind messaged Amelia.

We're going to be famous. Our pictures will be in the paper. Maybe we'll get on TV too.

Awesome. Except… Amelia messaged back.

For Mia, they thought at the same time.

"Fine," Mum was saying. "You'll be round at two? Yes, the girls will be ready. See you then."

"Mum!" Poppy wailed.

"Whatever is it?"

"Umm. Nothing."

"Poppy what's the matter? One minute you're all for it and the next you're looking as if you've taken a bite out of something nasty."

"She doesn't fancy being a celebrity. She wants to stay anonymous," Dad teased.

"Is that right? Have you changed your mind? If you have I can cancel the interview." Mum looked at Poppy but before she could say anything else Jake chimed in.

"Dad, what's an anon-y-mouse?"

"It's small and it's brown and it…" Dad picked Jake up and tickled him until he burst into gales of giggles which gave Poppy the chance to slip out of the room.

Mum says we can cancel, she messaged Amelia.

We don't have to. Mia won't come. Dad said it was okay but I'm sure her parents won't let her, Amelia replied.

If they even know about it. Most probably they'll be sleeping in their coffins and won't answer their phones. So it's going to be okay, Poppy messaged back.

Now that she didn't have to worry about Mia, Poppy was looking forward to being interviewed for the local paper. When Amelia arrived the two girls went upstairs to work out what they were going to say because no one was going to believe that two witches, a pair of ghosts, and a vampire girl had foiled Mr Jones and his gang.

As they finished agreeing on their story the doorbell rang. There was the sound of voices in the hall then Mum called, "Poppy, Amelia, the people from the newspaper are here, and so is Mia."

Poppy looked at Amelia. Amelia looked at Poppy. Somehow they had to warn Mia without any of the adults noticing.

In the living room a lady with a ponytail and dark-rimmed glasses was busy talking to Mia while a large man with a camera was chatting to Poppy's dad about football.

"Hi." The lady waved her hand. "I'm Annie Burgess. I was asking your friend Mia about the disco last night and now you're here we can start the interview properly."

"Umm…" Poppy was thinking desperately. "Do you want us to put on our costumes?"

"We looked really cool," Amelia added. "I can go and get mine. My house is down the road and Mia's is not too far either."

"No. We want you as you are, don't we Duncan? The angle is that you're three ordinary schoolgirls who, when faced with a really tricky situation, show how brave and resourceful they can be."

"Right, we'll leave you to get on with it," Mum said. "Come on Jake and Bernard."

"No wait a minute…" Poppy said.

Think of something, she messaged.

Shall I do a sleep spell?

Poppy shook her head.

Forgetting powder? No that won't work. Amelia thought. "Cup of tea?" she said.

Brilliant, Poppy messaged, giving her a thumbs up.

"Of course," Mum stopped halfway through

the door. "What would everyone like to drink?"

While Mum was taking their orders Poppy ran upstairs to consult *The Witches' Handbook*.

"What you want," the book said, "is on page 201. Be careful that you don't—"

"I won't." Poppy was too busy memorising the spell to listen. "Thank you," she called as she raced down the stairs chanting the words over and over again under her breath to make sure she remembered them.

Back in the living room everyone had their cup of tea or coffee or glass of juice. *It's okay, I can fix it,* Poppy messaged.

Amelia let out her breath and smiled but Mia was looking increasingly nervous and Poppy wished there was some way of letting her know that everything was going to be all right.

Annie put down her cup. "If you're ready shall we get started?"

"Sure," Poppy said brightly. "Shall we sit on the sofa, all three of us together?"

"That would make a great shot." Duncan started adjusting his camera.

Mia gave a gasp and glanced at the door. Poppy shook her head.

"Let's get the interview done first," Annie said. "The pictures can come later. I know you, Duncan, you'll be fussing around for ages." She took out her phone. "Who wants to go first?"

There was a pause. Mia started to get to her feet,

but Poppy put her hand on her friend's arm. The pause grew longer. Finally Amelia said, "I will."

"That's brilliant." Annie's smile was forced. "You were at the Halloween Disco and then…" she pressed record.

"Then we—" Amelia stopped.

A thin sliver of green slime trickled from Annie's phone.

"Then you…" Annie prompted. The slime thickened into a line of snot and coiled slowly down the journalists' arm,

"What the—" Annie leapt to her feet.

"Shall I get some tissues?" Poppy asked.

"I don't—"

Gobs of snot dripped onto the carpet.

"What's happening? What's going on?" Annie flung the phone away. It plopped on the ground with a plump squelch like a berry being squashed. "Duncan!" she shrieked.

"I told you, you should have upgraded." The photographer took out a huge handkerchief and picked up what was left of the mobile. "Can one of you girls bring a cloth to wipe up this mess?"

Keeping her hand down at her side so no one could see what she was doing, Poppy clicked her fingers.

"What mess?" Amelia asked innocently.

"The snot, the effluent, the green gunge." Annie was almost hysterical.

"Where? I can't see any." Mia joined in. "Except

for that bit running down the side of your face."

"Noooo!" Annie wailed.

Poppy jumped up from the sofa and handed Annie a box of tissues. "It's on the right, under your ear."

The journalist scrubbed furiously, then taking a mirror out of her bag examined every inch of her face.

"What do you want me to do with this?" Duncan held out the handkerchief with the phone wrapped in it.

"Throw it out. Get rid of it. Do what you like, only never, ever let it anywhere near me again."

"There's nothing wrong with it." Poppy clicked her fingers. "There might be a bit of green from that big sneeze you did but it looks okay to me."

"She's right." Duncan stared in amazement at the phone. "Give it a wipe and it'll be fine."

Annie shuddered. She took her phone and shoved it hastily into her bag.

"Sorry about that."

"About what?" the girls said.

"Oh, nothing. My phone isn't working so I'll um…"

"I'll get you something to write on," Poppy offered.

"Makes me feel like something out of the Dark Ages." Annie opened the notebook Poppy gave her. "Now—" she bit the top of her pen "—you were at the Halloween Disco when…"

"We saw something in the yard," Poppy took up the story. Together, with Mia and Amelia, she gave an account of what had happened leaving out the bits about ghosts and vampires.

"You were very brave," Annie said once they finished.

"Not really." Poppy looked at Amelia and Mia and they all shrugged.

Nothing can go wrong if you've got ghosts and a vampire on your side, she messaged Amelia who looked away to stop herself from giggling.

"Time for the photographs. If you girls can stand over there." Duncan picked up his camera.

"Me and Poppy will," Amelia said helpfully. "Mia can't have her picture taken."

"That's right," Mia said. "My mum and dad won't give their permission."

Duncan heaved a huge sigh. "Okay," he said through gritted teeth, "in that case it's just Poppy and Amelia. That's it, girls, arms around each other's shoulders and smile."

Chapter 17

A BARRAGE OF voices greeted Poppy and Amelia when they walked into the schoolyard on Monday morning. Phones came out and everyone wanted a picture of the girls that had saved the school from being burgled.

"What about Mia?" Will said. "She was there too, wasn't she?"

"Yes," Poppy said. "She'll tell you about it, but she's not here yet."

It wasn't until the bell had rung and 7C were lining up with the rest of their year that a large black car with heavily tinted windows drew up and Mia got out.

"I saw everyone taking pictures so I made Chris go back down the road and wait," Mia explained as she slipped into the line beside Poppy and Amelia.

At registration Mr Charles told them there was going to be a special assembly and the whole year was buzzing with excitement when 7C filed into the hall. Mrs Dunston walked on to the stage and there was an expectant hum, which quickly died away when the headteacher began speaking.

"As most of you know, on Friday night after the

Halloween Disco, there was a break in and if it had not been for three girls from 7C the school would have lost almost all our IT equipment. Luckily for us, Poppy Barrington, Amelia Reeves and Mia Delaney, showing the utmost courage and ingenuity, managed to foil the burglars. Come up here, girls, and let your year show their appreciation."

Mrs Dunston started to clap and the whole year joined in. As Poppy, followed by Amelia and Mia, walked up the steps the noise was almost deafening. Standing next to the headteacher, Poppy glanced at her friends. It was very strange being there while the rest of the year clapped and whooped and whistled, but it felt good.

Catching her thoughts, Amelia smiled back and even Mia managed a half-grin.

Mrs Dunston finally brought the applause to a halt and said, "If everyone behaved with as much forethought and bravery as the three of you the world would be a better place. I know you didn't do it for a reward but you will have ten house points each."

"Yeah!" someone yelled from the back of the hall and for once Mrs Dunston smiled instead of giving the shouter a detention.

The first lesson was science. The lab door was locked and they had to wait for Miss Mortimer to let them in. The room looked as if a hurricane had swept through it. Stools were turned upside down. Taps were turned on. Books and papers were thrown all over the place. Cupboards had been emptied and glassware broken.

And written all over the walls were the words, **I know what you are.**

"Never in the whole of my teaching career have I seen such a despicable mess," Miss Mortimer cried. "Whoever is responsible will be punished most severely." She glared at Poppy and Amelia, then turned to one of the boys. "Will, go and tell Mrs Dunston what has happened and we'll find another room for our lesson."

"Why was she looking at us?" Poppy whispered as they filed into an empty classroom.

"Cos she doesn't like you?" Mia said.

"She doesn't and I've got a bad feeling about this," Amelia said and in spite of the warm glow inside her, Poppy had to agree.

They were halfway through the lesson when there was a knock at the door. "Come in," Miss Mortimer said with a strange smile.

Poppy felt something twist inside her. She glanced at Amelia as a boy from 7R handed the teacher a note. Amelia shrugged and bit her lip.

"Poppy, Amelia and Mia you are to go to the headteacher's office immediately," Miss Mortimer said.

A murmur went round the class, but one look from Miss Mortimer and everyone fell silent.

"I wonder what Mrs Dunston wants," Poppy

said as they walked along the corridor to the headteacher's office.

"Perhaps more house points?" Mia suggested hopefully.

"Our pictures in the school newsletter?" Amelia said.

"A week off school as a reward?" To keep her mind off the uneasy feeling that was growing ever stronger, Poppy tried to think of the most outrageous rewards and privileges they could be given.

"We only have to go to the lessons we like."

"We can have chips for lunch every day, not just on Fridays." Amelia joined in.

"We'll always be allowed in first for dinner."

"We can go home whenever we want," Mia added.

"We can..." Amelia ran out of ideas as they reached the headteacher's office.

Poppy's nervousness spread between them like the flu and no one wanted to knock at the door. Mia was the first to pluck up courage.

"Come," Mrs Dunston called and they filed in. Unlike the smiles and congratulations at assembly the head's expression was grim. "I have been informed of the damage to Miss Mortimer's science room—" She paused. "Poppy, Amelia, Mia ... I am shocked and disappointed. Less than an hour ago you were being praised for your actions. Had I known what I know now it would have been a very different matter."

"What are we supposed to have done?" Poppy burst out.

Mrs Dunston sighed deeply. "Mr Charles tells ·me that you three girls were the last to leave the building after the disco. Miss Mortimer says there was nothing wrong with her room when she left school on Friday evening. The only pupils who had access to her classroom were the three of you."

"You think we trashed the science lab?" Amelia cried.

"I am afraid you were the only ones who could have done it. Everyone else had gone home."

"Mr Jones was there. So were Kyle and Nathan," Mia said, quietly.

"Mr Jones and his associates were too busy stealing the IT equipment." Mrs Dunston frowned. "I thought you were the sort of pupils that are a real credit to our school. Instead I find that you are three very silly girls who think smashing up a classroom is fun."

"We didn't do it!" Poppy protested.

"It's not fair!" Amelia cried.

"Enough!" The head held up her hand. "The three of you are excluded for two days. I have informed your parents and they are coming to take you home. Except for yours, Mia. My secretary tells me they cannot be reached."

That's cos they're asleep in their coffins. Even

though she felt wretched Poppy had to bite the inside of her cheek to stop herself from smiling.

"Since we can't get hold of them you will have to wait at school until the end of the day. In the meantime all three of you go and sit in the foyer. You will sit separately and not talk to each other or I will add another day to your exclusion."

Miss Mortimer has got something to do with this, Poppy messaged as they took their seats in the foyer.

Do you think she's put a spell on Mrs Dunston? Amelia replied.

Of course she has. Otherwise she'd have believed us when we said we didn't do it.

They both looked at Mia. The vampire girl sat with her head bowed, her hands in her lap, and looked so miserable that they wished they could message her too.

It was even worse when first Amelia's dad and then Poppy's came to fetch them and they had to leave Mia sitting there all alone until the end of the school day.

Mr Barrington didn't say a word as he and Poppy walked home. When they got in he made them both a drink and sat Poppy down at the kitchen table.

"Tell me the truth. Mrs Dunston said something about a lab being vandalised, but it doesn't sound like the sort of thing any of you girls would do."

"It wasn't us Dad."

"Why did Mrs Dunston say it was?"

"I don't know. It's not fair. We're being blamed for something we didn't do and we can't do anything about it."

"You don't know anything about what happened in the lab?"

"How could we? We were by the IT rooms on the other side of the school and before that we were locked in Mr Jones' storeroom. Besides, if we were vandalising the school we wouldn't have called the police, would we?"

"Did you say that to Mrs Dunston?"

"She wouldn't listen. Nobody listens."

"I'm listening."

Poppy nodded. "I thought you'd be cross, Dad."

"There was no point in being angry until I knew more."

"Now you do. Someone trashed the lab and me and Amelia and Mia got the blame."

"That's tough."

"Yes," Poppy growled.

"Sometimes these things happen and you have to deal with them."

"But we got excluded!"

"It could have been a lot worse. Look at it this way, you'll have some time off and the day after tomorrow you'll be back at school."

"I don't want to go. Ever again. Everyone will

think we did it." Poppy kicked at the chair with her heels. "Unless…"

"Unless what?"

"We prove that we didn't."

Dad grinned and passed Poppy the biscuits.

I DIDN'T GET into trouble, Poppy messaged later.

Nor me. I thought Dad would be furious but he believed me. Everyone believes us except Mrs Dunston.

And Miss Mortimer.

We'll show them.

Although they were not supposed to go anywhere near the school, Poppy and Amelia sneaked out to wait for Mia at the end of the day. She was the first to leave, walking across the yard with her head down, her shoulders slumped.

"It's all over," she told them. "Now I've got into trouble we'll have to move again."

"No you won't," Poppy said. "We were excluded too and no one says we have to change schools."

"You're not like me," Mia said sadly. "Once I'm noticed we're all in danger. Mrs Dunston already thinks it's strange that no one came to collect me. There's only so many excuses Chris and Hera can give for not coming to the school."

"We're not going to let you go," Poppy said. "As soon as we get back we're going to find out who was responsible."

ON THURSDAY MORNING Poppy and Mia met up at Amelia's house so the three of them could walk to school together. Although she was determined not to show it Poppy was nervous about going back after being excluded.

"It'll be all right," she said, partly to convince herself. "If anyone says anything they'll have all three of us to reckon with."

"We're like the Three Musketeers," Amelia said and they stopped in the middle of the pavement to give each other high fives, which made Poppy feel so much better she almost wished someone would start something.

"Hi," she said to the group of Year Sevens standing by the gates talking excitedly to each other. "What's going on?"

"Our classroom's been trashed," Will said.

"It wasn't you again, was it?" asked one of his friends.

"No it wasn't. We didn't do it in the first place." Poppy was furious.

"It wasn't a break in," Will continued. "Lily, the

crossing lady, says there was nothing on the security cameras."

"A mystery then," Poppy said. She turned to Mia and Amelia "Do you think Mrs Dunston will apologise for blaming us?"

"No chance," Amelia said. "Grownups never do that. If they think they're right they stay right. Or pretend they never got it wrong in the first place."

"If it wasn't a break in then who did it?" Poppy said as they lined up.

"Who or what?" Amelia said.

Mia nodded. "There's only one explanation – the school is being haunted."

Chapter 18

AS 7C FILED into the building the lights flickered and went out. Everyone shrieked and made ghostly noises.

"I said it was ghosts," Mia said.

At that moment the lights came back on. Amelia grabbed Poppy's arm and pointed to the girl at the other end of the corridor. She was about their age but instead of a school uniform she was wearing a long dress. Her hair was piled up on the top of her head.

"That's her. That's the ghost," Mia whispered.

"What's she doing here?" Poppy said.

"I don't know. We'll have to ask her."

No one else seemed to notice the girl but there was a chill in the air which grew colder as they approached her, and the rest of the class hurried past as fast as they could.

"Go on." Mia nudged Poppy in the ribs but before she could say anything Miss Mortimer appeared on the very spot where, only seconds before, they had seen the ghost.

"Hurry up. You don't want to be late for class on your first day back," Miss Mortimer said with a smirk, then turned and strode down the corridor as if appearing out of nowhere was nothing unusual.

"That's so weird," Amelia gasped.

"I knew it was something to do with her," Poppy hissed.

"Do you mean she brought the ghost here?"

"It looks like it," Mia agreed. "And Miss Mortimer's not going to let us talk to her."

"So…" Amelia said.

"We're going to have to come back tonight," Poppy said.

THERE WAS A frosty ring around the moon when Poppy climbed onto her broomstick and flew out of the bedroom window. Soaring up above the rooftops she was joined by Amelia. They landed in the schoolyard where Mia was waiting for them.

"What are we going to do?" Amelia asked. The building was dark except for the red glow of the security light. "We can't see in and we can't get in."

"We could, um … wait?" Now that they'd arrived Poppy had ran out of ideas.

"No need for that dears." In a wisp of white, two ghosts appeared. "Mia told us about your problem," Granny said. "Mmm—" she frowned "—I can sense it. There's a thinning in the fabric of time. It's round here somewhere."

"It's a portal," Grandpa nodded. "That's where your ghost has been coming and going. Someone has left it open and it's been slipping through. It's very unusual. I can't remember the last time we came across anything like it. Can you?"

"No," Granny said vaguely and floated round the side of the building.

"Take care of each other," Grandpa said. "It's best if you hold hands. Going through time can be very disturbing especially if you've not done it before."

Poppy grabbed Mia's hand. Mia took Amelia's and they hurried after Granny. They'd only gone a few steps when the ground beneath their feet turned spongey and the air began to tremble. The stars flickered like lights being switched on and off. The glow of the streetlamps disappeared and when they turned the corner, the school wasn't there.

"Where's it gone?" Poppy stared at the mansion in front of them.

"It hasn't gone anywhere. It's not been built yet. I told you we were going back in time and here we are," Granny said.

"Awesome," Amelia breathed.

"Absolutely awesome," Poppy echoed.

"It's like something out of a painting." Mia

gazed at the house, its windows glowing with candlelight. A full moon hung above the trees that surrounded the grounds and a shaft of silver light fell across the path where a girl was hurrying towards them.

"It's her. It's the ghost," Poppy said.

"What do we do?" Amelia asked.

"Talk to her of course. That's why we're here. Hi!" Mia waved her hand.

"Go away. Don't come near me." The girl made a cross with her fingers and held them in front of her face.

"We're not going to hurt you." Poppy took a step forward.

The girl shrank back. "How do I know that? You're demons, all of you. The lady with the beaky nose and dark hair warned me that you'd come to haunt me."

"We're not haunting you," Amelia said. "You're haunting our school."

"What do you mean?"

"The place where you go and throw all our stuff around and break things. That's Ashley Park School," Amelia said.

"No it isn't. It's a portal to the land of demons. She said so. She said I must destroy their works."

"We're not demons," Amelia said. "We're…" She hesitated, trying to work out what would frighten the girl the least.

"I know what you are." The girl pointed at Mia.

"You are a vampire – like Louis."

"Yes I am," Mia said calmly. "Poppy and Amelia are human and they are also witches."

"Good ones," Poppy said quickly. "Not like Miss Mortimer."

"The woman with the beaky nose and black hair," Amelia explained.

"I am completely confused," the girl cried. "She – your Miss Mortimer – told me that there was great danger and the only way to save those I care about was to do as she said. But if you're the danger..."

"We're not," Amelia said.

"You don't look like demons," the girl said slowly.

"And you know what vampires are like. If you want you can always ask Louis," Mia said.

"Do you know him? Oh—" the girl hesitated "—how rude of me. I am Catherine Lacey. Louis is a friend of my brother Jacob."

"We're Poppy, Amelia and Mia," Poppy said. "And we come from the twenty-first century."

"The twenty-first century! How can this be possible?"

"We came here the same way you come to our time, through the portal Miss Mortimer opened. She wants you to get us into trouble."

"She hates us because we won't join her coven," Amelia said. "So we came to ask you to stop."

"I wish I could but I cannot," Catherine sighed.

"Why not?" Amelia asked.

"It's a long story." Catherine glanced warily over her shoulder. "I cannot tell you here. Come to my room and we can talk there."

"Won't someone see us?"

"I had not thought of that."

"No problem. Go upstairs and open your window as wide as it will go," Poppy said.

Catherine returned to the house and when the three girls saw her opening the shutters Mia hopped onto the back of Poppy's broomstick; Amelia mounted hers and they flew up to the window. Catherine welcomed them in and after they'd made themselves comfortable on the four-poster bed she drew the curtains so that it was like sitting in a tent of green silk. Then she began her story.

"At the end of the summer my brother Jacob returned from a voyage to Louisiana with his friend Louis, who was in a great deal of trouble." Catherine lowered her voice. "He had turned the daughter of a very important man into a vampire. They loved each other and it was the only way they could be together. When her father discovered what they had done he was furious. He locked up his daughter and sent vampire hunters after Louis.

"Jacob thought he would be safe in England. But Miss Mortimer came and said that unless I destroy the demons they would lead the vampire hunters here and poor Louis would have a stake thrust through the heart and shrivel into dust." Mia shuddered. "Jacob would be arrested and put on trial for conjuring an evil spirit and could be hanged for his crime. I could not let that happen so I did what she told me. I summoned up my courage and went through the portal and did my best to destroy it. I am sorry if it caused trouble for you but what else can I do? If I protect Louis and Jacob then you suffer. If I do not then—"

"Please. I don't want to talk about it," Mia said quickly.

"It's not going to happen. We'll think of something." Poppy looked at her friends.

Amelia frowned and shook her head. The four girls sat in silence until suddenly there was a clatter of hooves. Catherine leapt up, pulled back the bed curtains, and ran to the window.

A party of horsemen came galloping down the drive and drew to a halt in front of the house. Their leader dismounted, strode up the steps, and banged loudly on the door. "Open up. We have come to destroy that unnatural creature you harbour," he shouted.

"It's the vampire hunters," Catherine cried. "They must have followed you. I should never, ever have believed you. Louis will be taken away and Jacob hanged, and it is my doing."

"Stop it," Poppy said.

"It wasn't us. Mia is a vampire and she's our

best friend, so why would we bring the vampire hunters here?" Amelia said.

"I do not know. All I know is that I must find Louis and warn him before it is too late."

"Let us in, or we will knock down your door," one of the hunters cried.

"Where's Louis?" Poppy asked.

"He could be in the park. It is dinner time and he never eats with the family. Of course Jacob and I know why, but he tells Mamma and Papa, that delicious though the food is he has no appetite and will take the air."

"And if he's not in the grounds where else could he be?" Mia asked.

"He could be up on the roof, but even there he may not be safe, not if they search the house thoroughly. What are we going to do?"

"You stay here. Me and Amelia will fly round the park and Mia will check the roof. If you can think of anything to distract the hunters that would be good."

As Poppy and Amelia flew out of the window, the door of the mansion opened and Mr Lacey walked out onto the steps.

"What is this disturbance? I know nothing of any unnatural being," he said.

"Then give us leave to enter and search your premises."

"On whose authority?"

"The Justice of the Peace. We have a warrant

here."

"Very well. Let me see it."

"Papa, have they come to deal with the ghost in the old nursery?" Catherine ran out to join her father.

"I think, my dear, it is more than a ghost that has brought these gentlemen here."

"But that ghost is very troublesome. It frightens me and…"

Poppy and Amelia did not stay to hear anymore. Catherine was buying them time. Now they had to find Louis and then return to the twenty-first century as quickly as they could.

Chapter 19

THE NIGHT WAS much darker than anything Poppy and Amelia were used to. There were no streetlights, only the moon and the weak light spilling out from the door of the mansion. After the door had been closed, leaving only the moonlight, it took a few moments for their eyes to adjust to the gloom.

In front of them, the drive curved down to the gates, running past clumps of trees and a small white building which looked like a Greek temple.

We can try over there, Poppy messaged.

"There's no one here. There's no light on," Amelia said when they landed.

"A vampire wouldn't need lights. Mia can see in the dark. I'm going in." Poppy's hand was on the doorknob when Amelia gave a muffled gasp.

"You are quite correct. A vampire needs no light," said a voice.

Poppy whirled round and saw a cloaked figure with his arm around Amelia's neck.

"Do not scream or raise the alarm. If you do this lad will pay the price. It will not take long to drain his blood. I have not feasted for a while and I am very hungry." The vampire lowered his head and bared his fangs.

"Leave her alone! Let her go! We don't mean you any harm. We came to warn you."

"You are lying. You are in league with the hunters. Why else would you say this lad is a girl when he is dressed as boy?"

"Because she is a girl. She's wearing jeans. We both are. Look, I can explain but not now. You have to get away from here or they'll find you."

"How can I trust you?"

"Because they're my friends." Mia landed in front of them. In the distance they could hear the vampire hunters shouting instructions, their lanterns bobbing in the darkness as they poured out of the house to search the grounds.

"Catherine and her brother couldn't hold them any longer. Why didn't you go up on the roof? It may have been safer there."

"It might indeed but I had no idea that they would catch up with me tonight. I came to the summer house as usual, pleading a headache."

"So you wouldn't have to eat dinner," Poppy said.

"She knows our ways." Louis loosened his hold on Amelia who gulped and took deep breaths of air.

"We have to go. They're getting closer. But I can't..." Mia swayed.

She's too tired to fly, Poppy thought.

"Don't worry little one." Louis's fangs grazed

Mia's neck. She shuddered, threw her arms out wide and … disappeared. A small bat hovered above their heads, joined almost instantly by a larger one. The bats circled the summer house before flying off into the night sky.

"They're safe," Poppy said.

"We're not." Amelia pointed to the men racing towards them.

"Hey you there. Stop!" one cried.

"Let's go." Poppy mounted her broomstick. Amelia did the same and they soared up above the park.

Find Mia, Poppy messaged.

Where do we look?

On the roof? It's where Louis might go to hide. Then we can all go back to our own time.

Amelia's broomstick wobbled as she was struck by a horrible thought. The only way home was through the portal and that was near the house where the vampire hunters were sure to see them.

As her friends headed for the mansion, up on the roof Mia transformed into her own shape. After being a bat her legs felt heavy, her arms too long for her body. Her head was fuzzy and filled with high pitched squeaks. "I feel dizzy," she said.

"Sit down and rest," Louis said. "It can take you like that the first time. Especially if you have not been prepared."

"Chris and Hera – they are my parents – said I

was too young. They said that transforming into a bat would be something I'd be able to do as I got older."

"This was an emergency, and you managed well. Did you say you are a child of vampires? I have never met one so young before. They are very rare. Your makers, I mean your parents, are very privileged."

"They wouldn't think so. They're not that keen on being vampires. They'd rather I was a natural, I mean normal human being like they used to be."

"That is not a path open to us." There was a hint of sadness in Louis' voice that make Mia wonder if he regretted being a vampire, but this was not the time to ask him.

Mentioning her parents, however, gave her an idea. "Louis, you are in danger here. Why don't you come with us?"

"I thank you for the offer but it will make no difference. Once they are on my trail the vampire hunters will follow wherever I go. After we left Louisiana, Jacob assured me that I would be safe in his family home in England, provided of course that I did not feast on human blood."

"And you didn't?"

There was a long pause.

"Okay, but if you come back to my time you must promise you'll never do that again."

"Your time?" Louis looked startled.

"We're from the twenty-first century." Poppy

and Amelia landed on the tiles.

"You are telling tales. Travelling through time is impossible. I should never have transformed you, Mia. It has unhinged your mind."

"We're not mad." Amelia pulled her phone out of her pocket. "See." She lit up the screen.

"What magic is this?"

"It's a phone. We use it to speak to each other when we are not in the same place. I can't show you right now because there isn't a signal."

"Why would the Laceys be sending a signal? We are not at sea," Louis said.

"Phones are not the only things," Poppy said. "We have cars and airplanes so we can fly anywhere we want in the world. And there is the internet and toilets and—" She stopped. Louis was looking more and more confused.

"Don't worry, you'll learn. And you won't starve. Chris gets regular supplies from the blood banks," Mia told him.

"You have banks for blood as well as money? Now I have heard everything. The twenty-first century is truly a land of enchantment."

"Then you'll come?"

"How could I not? What is there here for me but an endless flight from insatiable enemies?"

The trap door to the roof opened and Catherine and her brother climbed out. "Thank goodness you are safe, Louis," Catherine cried.

"He'll be safer still when he comes with us,"

Poppy said.

"Are you leaving?" Jacob looked at his friend.

"I have little choice. The vampire hunters have left but they will be back. The danger here is too great and my remaining puts both of you in mortal peril."

"Much as it will pain me never to see you again, perhaps it is for the best." Jacob's eyes were full of tears.

"My dear, dear friend—" Louis gave Jacob a hug "—could I not persuade you to join me?" His fangs glinted in the moonlight.

"No you can't," Poppy and Amelia said together.

"It would mess with everything," Mia said.

"Then go and do not forget us. Goodbye, Louis," Jacob said.

Catherine promised never to visit Ashley Park School again and Jacob watched in astonishment as she jumped onto Poppy's broomstick. Amelia climbed onto hers and Mia and Louis transformed into bats. They flew down from the roof to the place where Poppy, Amelia and Mia had first entered the eighteenth century.

"This has been the most exciting day of my life. I am truly sorry that it will be the last time we meet," Catherine said.

"We could come and see you," Poppy said.

"No we couldn't. It would be too complicated. Sorry about that." Amelia gave Catherine a quick hug.

Then the bats transformed into human shape and they all turned towards the portal. They moved carefully, expecting at any moment that the ground would turn spongey and the air begin to tremble as the fabric of time thinned enough for them to slip through.

After a while Poppy stopped. "Something's wrong. I'm sure the portal wasn't this far from the house."

"It wasn't." Amelia frowned. "Miss Mortimer must have closed it. She's always wanted to get rid of us and now she has."

Chapter 20

"YOU MEAN WE'RE stuck here?" Poppy's insides flipped.

"Looks like it. Unless we can think of another way to get home." Amelia swallowed a sob. Louis shrugged. Mia frowned and shook her head.

Poppy clutched her broomstick. "Shame we can't fly back." She tried a grin but her mouth wouldn't do what she wanted. The thought that she might never see Mum and Dad and Jake and Bernard again made her want to cry.

"Isn't there some magic you can do?" Mia sounded equally desperate.

"I didn't get to that bit in the handbook," Amelia said.

"If it's even in the book. Why would witches want to go back to the past? Mostly it was a really bad time for them," Poppy said.

"They must be able to do it though, seeing as Miss Mortimer opened the portal," Mia said.

"I wish—" Poppy began.

"That's it, we can wish ourselves back. The only thing is, the handbook says that for really serious magic we need wands," Amelia said. "Which we haven't got," she added gloomily.

"My dear young ladies," said Louis, "are you telling me that you are witches without wands? Surely there is an abundance of twigs and branches all around you. You have only to select something suitable and say a spell or two, and abracadabra, you will have wands."

"How come you're an expert on magic?" Poppy asked.

"I have over the centuries encountered many a witch. They, like us vampires, have also been unjustly persecuted."

"Witches don't drink human blood."

"That is not our fault. That is how we are made," Louis retorted.

"Stop it!" Mia said. "This isn't getting us anywhere. Is Amelia right? Could you do the magic if you had wands?"

"I think so."

"Yes."

Amelia and Poppy spoke together.

"Then go for it and hurry. It's getting lighter and Louis will have to shelter after the sun comes up. There are no sunglasses or sunblock here."

How do we do this? Poppy messaged.

Clear your mind and think wands. Amelia shut her eyes and let her arms fall to her sides. Her broomstick leaned against her and she heard its twigs rustle.

"My broom says we need an older … no … an elder tree."

"Which one's an elder?"

"The ignorance of youth is astounding." Louis gave an exaggerated sigh. "There is a grove of elders over there."

Poppy and Amelia jumped on their broomsticks and headed for the middle of the clump of trees. As soon as their feet were on the ground their brooms twisted out of their grasp. They stood upright and began to sway and as they did so the trees moved in unison. The rhythm of the trees vibrated through the earth like an electric current. It travelled up from the ground through the girls' feet, their legs, their bodies, their arms and into their hands, tingling through their fingers as they were drawn to a pair of young elders.

"Will you let me have one of your twigs for a wand? I promise to look after it and keep it special the whole of my life," Poppy spoke first.

"Together we will do magic, not only for ourselves but also for the good of others," Amelia said.

The trees trembled. The dry sound of twigs was like the chatter of excited voices as they consulted and debated until finally a long drawn out "Yesss" whispered through the grove. A twig, the perfect size for a wand, fell into Poppy's hand and she felt its magic seep through her skin.

"It's like you are part of me," she whispered.

"Like you've always been mine," Amelia

murmured holding the twig she had been given.

The trees around them sighed. A soft wind blew through the grove like a blessing and Poppy and Amelia knew they were part of the earth and its magic.

I never want to leave here, Poppy thought.

This is where we belong, Amelia replied.

"Hey, are you two all right? You look really dozy?" Mia came running towards them.

"We're okay." Amelia blinked and tightened her grip on her wand.

"We really are," Poppy added. "I feel as if I could do anything. It's absolutely—"

"Awesome," Amelia said.

"Then get us home and do it now." Mia cast an anxious glance at the thin line of light along the horizon.

"Hold hands and hold on to our brooms." Poppy raised her wand. "Take us back," she murmured.

"To our own time," Amelia joined in.

"Back, back through the portal," they chanted.

"Through the portal," Mia echoed.

A shaft of sun spread its rays across the sky. The trees whispered and murmured, the ground wavered, the air rushed through and past them, knocking them off their feet, sending them whirling and twirling until with a sudden bump they were standing in the schoolyard.

"That was amazing!" Poppy said.

Louis looked up at the sky. "This is a place of magic. The sky is lit up even at night. Where are the stars? Is this indeed the future, or some Faerie Realm?"

"It's England and we have to move fast." Mia was texting. "I've told my dad to come and fetch us before daybreak. We can't let anyone see you," she said to the bewildered looking vampire.

"Not dressed like that," Poppy said.

"Not now that Halloween is over," Amelia said.

"Halloween? What I pray is that?"

The three girls looked at each other. There was going to be a lot of explaining to do if Louis was going to fit into the twenty-first century.

There was a whoosh of air and Chris appeared in front of them. "Welcome, sir," he bowed his head to Louis. "I am Mia's father and if you will follow me I will take you to a place where you will be safe. Mia are you coming with us?" He gave his daughter a look which meant she had no choice. Though Mia raised her eyebrows and sighed she took her dad's hand and the three vampires flew out of the schoolyard and away over the rooftops.

Chapter 21

POPPY AND AMELIA reached home just in time to get ready for school.

"I think I need another staying-awake spell," Poppy groaned when the three girls met up at the school gates.

"No you don't. We don't want to go through that again," Amelia said. "You were so cross and horrible."

"That's cos everything was wrong and it still is." Poppy scuffed her shoe against the tarmac.

"No it isn't. We rescued Louis and Miss Mortimer's plan didn't work."

"Neither did ours. Everyone still thinks we trashed the classrooms and we can't prove we didn't because who's going to believe it was a ghost."

"They will." Mia's lips curved upwards. "You'll see."

They followed the rest of their class into registration … and as soon as they sat down at their desks it began. First, Poppy's backpack rose from the floor and floated over to the door. Then Amelia's pencil case darted around the room. As 7C gasped and shrieked bags opened and books and folders rose into the air.

"What's going on?" Mr Charles cried, dodging a packet of pens. "Who's throwing things?"

"No one sir," Mia said. "Show him everyone." She put her hands in the air and not wanting to be blamed for something they weren't doing, 7C followed suit.

"Then what is it?" Mr Charles brushed aside Will's sandwich box which was aiming straight for his ear.

"Poltergeists or ghosts, or both," Mia said looking at the back of the room where Granny and Grandpa Ghost were having great fun teleporting the contents of 7C's school bags.

"How do we stop it?"

"I don't know. Maybe it will go away." Mia nodded to the ghosts who grinned and vanished through the wall. "They're going to Mrs Dunston's office next," she whispered to her friends as everyone began retrieving their belongings. "Then they might visit a few more classrooms."

"Mia—" Poppy looked at her with admiration. "—that was awesome."

"Absolutely awesome," Amelia added.

Mia shrugged. "It was the least I could do for my friends."

By the end of the day everyone was talking about the haunting of Ashely Park School. Mrs Dunston called Poppy, Amelia and Mia into her office to apologise for wrongly accusing them and told them that she had called in a ghost hunter to clear the building of unwanted spirits.

Poppy walked out of Mrs Dunston's room feeling much better than she had that morning … until she saw Miss Mortimer. The science teacher gave them such a baleful look that Poppy clutched Amelia's arm. Amelia gave a gasp and Mia half-bared her teeth. Miss Mortimer might have failed to get rid of them this time but they were sure she would try again.

For the next few days they were very careful to keep out of her way, but when nothing happened they began to relax.

On Saturday morning Poppy and Amelia received invitations to a party at Barbara's house. Poppy's dad agreed to drive them to Broome Compton, the village where Barbara's family lived, but there was one problem.

What are we going to do about Mia? We said we'd go and see her and find out how Louis is getting on. We can't let her down, Amelia messaged.

No we can't. Poppy was looking forward to seeing Barbara and the other girls from the Flying Broomstick Academy but they couldn't let a friend down. Unless…

I'll ask if she can come too.

She texted Barbara, who replied that Mia was welcome so long as she had some magic.

She can turn into a bat, Poppy texted back and

Barbara said in that case it was fine and she'd see them all later.

IT WAS DRIZZLING as they set off for the party. Outside the city the rain began to fall more heavily. Huge puddles spread across the lanes. In some places the water was so deep it was like driving through a pond. By the time they reached Broome Compton they had slowed to a crawl.

Poppy's dad was worried. "I don't think I should leave you here," he said, pulling up in front of Willow Cottage.

"We'll be okay, Dad."

"The river looks as if it's going to flood and if it does we won't be able to come and fetch you."

"Then we'll stay at Barbara's. We can sleep on the floor. It'll be fun." Poppy couldn't tell her dad that she and Amelia had their broomsticks with them and Mia could easily fly home, either as a vampire or a bat.

"All right—" Mr Barrington made up his mind "—off you go and have a good time."

Poppy watched her dad inch back down the lane and wished she had a spell to take him safely home.

"He'll be all right and if he isn't we can always

go and rescue him on our broomsticks," Amelia said.

The thought of Dad clinging on behind her as they flew back to Raleigh Road made Poppy giggle and she was still laughing as the three girls walked up the path to Willow Cottage. They were about to knock when the letterbox flapped open.

"Come in," said a voice. They looked around but there was no one there.

"Is it magic?" Mia asked.

"It's the letterbox opening its big mouth before you even knocked." A small black cat with yellow eyes glared at them. "I'm Ivy, Barbara's sister. Go on in. They know you're coming." The cat curled her tail over her back and sauntered away.

"What about you?" Poppy said.

"Don't bother about her." Barbara was at the door, a large tabby cat at her side. "She's having one of her strops. The rest of us are here already so park your broomsticks by the door and let the party begin."

The inside of Willow Cottage was decked with garlands of evergreens. Red, orange, and purple candles stood on the windowsills and on the mantelpiece above the inglenook fireplace. Two cats, one black and white, the other a sleek grey, stretched out in front of the fire. A weasel and a couple of ferrets were curled up together and a toad squatted sleepily on the hearth.

"They're our familiars," Barbara said. "This is

Charlie." She bent down to stroke the tabby cat. "He's mine."

"I haven't got a familiar," Amelia said.

"Nor me." Poppy looked at the creatures clustered around the fire and wondered how Mum and Dad would react if she said she wanted a pet of her own. And what about Bernard? How would he get on with a new and magical creature?

"I'm sure you will one day," Barbara said encouragingly. "When it's the right time your familiar will turn up. That's how it happens."

"Familiars are really important." Vivica didn't even bother to say hello. "In our family we have Norwegian Forest Cats. Bonzo's mine. He's over there on the sofa. He's very big and fierce and he cost more than you would believe."

"Shut up, Vivica." Primrose approached. "You don't have to go on about all the stuff you've got."

"Not with us anyway." Su Lin accompanied by a lilac-pointed Siamese joined them. "Stay cool and have fun."

"Who do the ferrets belong to?" Mia asked.

"Fergie and Frenzil are mine," Primrose said proudly.

"They're so cute." Mia smiled flashing her teeth. It was great not having to pretend to be ordinary.

Amelia wanted to ask about the toad but Vivica, sensing the other girls weren't impressed by Bonzo, changed the subject. "So you're a vampire," she said to Mia. "My parents used know a couple of vampires. Of course they didn't stick around for long—"

"Your parents or the vampires?" Poppy said wickedly.

"The vampires had some trouble with the neighbours and anyway we moved into a bigger house, with more room for my pony."

"You're doing it again." Primrose raised her eyes.

Vivica scowled but Barbara clicked her fingers and music poured through the room and the party began. They danced and chatted and were about to organise broomstick races around the garden, even though it was still raining, when a bell sounded and Barbara's mother called, "Food's ready."

They trooped into the dining room where the table had been set with plates of everyone's favourite party food. There were pizzas, sausages, cakes, jellies, and big bowls of crisps.

"Enjoy," Barbara's mother said. "I don't want any leftovers."

They piled their plates and found somewhere to sit: Poppy, Amelia and Su Lin on the floor, Vivica on the sofa with Bonzo, while Barbara shared a footstool with Primrose.

"We've been busy getting ready all day. Mum and Aunt Mortimer…" Barbara was saying.

Am I hearing that? Poppy turned her head so

sharply that the room spun – and then everything went fuzzy. "Amelia, I feel so…" Her tongue wouldn't form the words. Her eyes were growing heavy, her head falling forward…

Mia standing by the table, still trying to decide whether to risk another cheese and onion crisp, saw plates slide off laps and glasses tumble to the ground as, one by one, all the other girls fell asleep.

The fire died. The room became cold. The candles sputtered and went out. The door opened and Miss Mortimer swept in. Mia didn't wait. Transforming into a bat she flew past the witch and out into the hall.

"This way." The letterbox raised its flap and Mia flew out and onto the roof where a small black cat was sitting washing its face.

"Ivy," Mia squeaked.

"I don't speak bat," the cat said.

And I don't speak cat. Mia transformed into a girl. "Ivy there's an emergency."

"Don't tell me it's Aunt Mortimer up to her tricks again. I thought it was strange when she offered to organise a party for Barbara. I told the parents but would they listen? No. Every time Aunt Mortimer comes to stay she does something evil, but Mum never learns. My parents are too nice. What's she done this time?"

"I don't know. I'm not a witch but everyone's fallen asleep."

"She's put them into a trance. That's easy to fix." The black cat leapt from the roof onto a wall then onto the ground. Mia, in bat shape, followed. "In we go." Ivy dived at the cat flap and was knocked backwards as the flap stayed shut. "She's locked it," the black cat hissed. "She can't do this." Ivy twisted her body and changed into a girl with spiky black hair, black-rimmed eyes, and a stud through her nose. She was dressed completely in black with black lipstick and nail varnish.

Marching up to the front door, Ivy grabbed the handle and sprang back with a yelp as a bolt of magic flowed through her palms. Next she tried the windows. This time she was flung into the air before sitting down with a bump.

"She's evil," Ivy snarled. "She's locked down the whole cottage. We can't get in and no one can get out. But why? She's done some pretty vile things before but never as bad as this."

"It's because of us. Or rather Poppy and Amelia. She must have organised the party to lure them here. She'll do anything to get rid of them because they stood up to her."

"Aunt Mortimer wouldn't like that."

"Can you stop her?"

"I'm not strong enough. Not on my own. If Mum and Dad are also asleep we're going to need a really powerful witch to break this spell. You don't know any, do you?"

"I'm a vampire." Mia held out her hands.

"What do I know?"

"What about your friends' families. Can they help?"

Mia shook her head. Poppy and Amelia's parents were humans with no magical talents. The only person she could think of was Mrs Harrison.

THE RAIN WAS slanting down and a fierce wind buffeted the small bat as she fought her way through the storm. By the time she reached Laburnum Avenue she was so tired all she could do was flop down on a windowsill and give a feeble squeak. A marmalade cat jumped up beside her and curled a claw around her wing.

"I'm a bat not a mouse," Mia squeaked. The cat took no notice and with the last of her strength she transformed back into a girl.

Marmaduke leapt backwards and slid to the ground.

"I didn't mean to startle you." Mia scrambled off the sill. "Turning into a bat was the only way I could get here and it's really, really urgent, so can I come in?"

The cat, who did not like losing his dignity, gave her an offended look.

"Please," Mia continued, "Poppy and Amelia

are in terrible trouble and Mrs Harrison is the only person that can help."

Marmaduke meowed and, winding his tail around her legs, escorted Mia to the door and dived through the cat flap. Almost immediately the door opened and Mrs Harrison was there to welcome Mia inside.

The workroom was warm and cosy. The air smelled of cinnamon and nutmeg. Mia started to speak but Mrs Harrison made her sit down and handed her a drink that smelled so delicious that Mia couldn't resist.

"No one was harmed in the procuring of this blood," the witch said after Mia drained the last drop. "It won't hurt you either and since you are feeling much better you can tell me all about this emergency of yours."

After Mia finished telling her what had happened Mrs Harrison narrowed her eyes, tut-tutted loudly and said, "Mortimer has outreached herself this time, but with my help you can remove her spell."

The witch took two bottles from her shelves. One was filled with a bright-red liquid, the other was a vivid green. She poured them into a third bottle and, murmuring some magic words, swirled the potions together. Strands of green and red twisted around each other but did not merge.

"Sprinkle this on the sleepers and they will wake."

"But I can't get into the house."

"You'll think of something. A vampire and a witch make a great team."

Mrs Harrison looked so fierce that Mia hardly dared to ask, but thinking of the danger her friends were in she said, "How am I going to carry a bottle?"

"Hmm!" Mrs Harrison snorted. She tied a thin skein of silk around the neck of the bottle, made a loop and clicked her fingers. As Mia transformed the bottle shrank until it was the perfect size for a bat to wear around its neck.

"Off you go." Mrs Harrison opened the door and waved Mia away. Marmaduke stalked off to settle himself by the fire.

The wind howled driving the rain into icy shards that weighed down her wings, but Mia flew on and on until she saw the lights of Broom Compton.

"Took you long enough." Ivy shook the raindrops from her hair.

"I'm here now, aren't I?" Mia was soaking wet, her arms ached, and she had to rub the numbness from her fingers before she could untie the bottle from around her neck. She had no idea how they were going to get it into the cottage until Ivy scrambled up the branches of the wisteria and onto the roof. Holding the potion, Mia leapt up to join her.

"We'll pour it down the chimney," Ivy said.

"The fire's died right down and even if it hasn't, a few drops of potion won't harm it. The heat will evaporate it and spread it through the cottage."

"Ivy, you're a star."

"I can't help being brilliant," Ivy said. "Get on with it. It's freezing up here."

Mia uncorked the bottle and leaning against the chimney emptied its contents down the flue. There was a crackle, a spit, and a volley of emerald, scarlet, indigo, orange and violet sparks shot into the sky.

"That should do it," Ivy said.

Inside the cottage a noise like an alarm clock followed by the whining of a drill shrilled through Poppy's head. She sat up, dislodging Amelia who had fallen asleep against her.

"I've got jelly in my hair."

"There's pizza on your nose."

"I'm sitting on a sausage."

"What's going on?"

All around them the other witches were waking up.

"Let us in." Mia tapped at the window.

"I'm coming." Poppy was getting to her feet when Miss Mortimer marched into the room muttering a string of magic words.

The two cats by the fire leapt up. Tails bristling, whiskers quivering, Jaspar and Willow flung themselves at the witch. With a meowl Charlie raced in from the hall and dug his claws into Miss

Mortimer's leg. As she screamed and stamped, Bonzo and the other familiars threw themselves into the fray.

"Get off me you horrible creatures," Miss Mortimer cried, flailing her arms. Her attackers hissed and yowled and bit and scratched until Barbara's parents came storming in.

"It's all right. Ambrose and I are awake. We'll deal with my sister," Barbara's mother said and keeping their eyes on Miss Mortimer the animals drew back.

"This time, Mortimer, you have gone too far," Ambrose said.

Miss Mortimer shrugged. "There's no harm done. Belinda, Ambrose, all I wanted was those two," she pointed to Poppy and Amelia. "The rest of you would have woken up and not remembered a thing."

"Poppy and Amelia are our guests," Barbara's father said sternly.

"And my friends." Mia banged on the window.

"We're still locked out." Ivy kicked furiously at the door.

"Open the door. Unlock the cottage," Ambrose ordered.

"And promise that you will never do anything like this again," Belinda said.

For a moment it looked as if Miss Mortimer was wavering. Then she stuck her nose in the air and said, "Make me."

"Very well, you asked for it. Come everyone." Barbara's mother held out her hands and they formed a circle around Miss Mortimer.

"Blood and bone turn to stone," Belinda began and round and round they went, chanting the spell. Willow, Jaspar and the other familiars, traced their own ring around the witches. Every time Miss Mortimer tried to break free they hissed and spat driving her back into the centre as the circle spun faster and the words of the spell grew more and more powerful.

Miss Mortimer covered her face with her arms and shrank to the ground, curling up smaller and smaller until at last she was nothing but a round shape on the carpet.

Barbara's mother's eyes flashed. Breaking the circle she pointed and a streak of white light spiralled from her fingers. There was the faintest groan then all that was left of Miss Mortimer was a small grey pebble. Barbara picked it up, opened a window, and flung it out onto the drive.

"At last," Ivy snarled, turning back into a cat. Running out into the garden she found the spot where the pebble had fallen, lifted her tail and peed.

Chapter 22

ON MONDAY MORNING when Miss Mortimer didn't turn up at school the rumour quickly spread that she had been sacked. No one knew why and of course and Poppy, Amelia and Mia couldn't tell anyone what had really happened to the science teacher.

Without Miss Mortimer to worry about the rest of the term passed smoothly. Mr Harrison came to teach in her place and to everyone's surprise he kept his classes in order and 7C were soon enjoying his lessons.

"The magic can't have been doing him any good," Poppy decided, and Mia and Amelia agreed.

Now, at the start of the Christmas holidays, Poppy was wondering what she could buy for Mia. Choosing presents for Amelia was easy because they had known each other since nursery and liked the same sort of things, but she had no idea what Mia did when she wasn't with them. Did she spend the time asleep in a coffin before going out at night with her parents? Or did they all stay at home with Granny and Grandpa Ghost?

I expect she reads books cos she's good at English.

Or plays games on her tablet cos she's good at IT and maths. But that doesn't help much. Poppy was about to message Amelia for inspiration when a big black bird tapped on her window. It looked very bedraggled and weary, as if it had flown a long way through rough weather and Poppy couldn't help feeling sorry for it. Opening the window a crack she told it to stay where it was and she'd go and get some bread.

"Thank you," said the bird. "If you don't mind, I'd like to come in."

"I didn't know I spoke bird," Poppy said.

"You must do otherwise you wouldn't understand me." The bird fluffed up its feathers. "It's freezing out here and I've got a message for you."

"For me?" Poppy was so astonished that she did as the bird asked and opened the window wider.

"There's one for your friend Amelia too."

The bird flew in and perched on the top of Poppy's wardrobe. Hunched over, its black eyes gleaming, its yellow beak sharp, it looked so sinister that Poppy was beginning to wish she'd left it outside.

"Who's the message from?" Poppy asked while at the same time messaging Amelia to come over straightaway.

"From the Grand Convention of Witches. They've been keeping an eye on you — and you," the bird said as Amelia flew in on her broomstick. "Don't worry, you haven't done anything wrong."

I don't like this, Amelia messaged. The bird turned its head and looked at her and she stared back. "What does the Grand Convention want with us?"

"To tell you how pleased they are with your progress. For two apprentice witches who do not come from a witching background, you have done very well indeed. So well that you have earned your Level One certificate in spell making and witchcraft."

"Do they want us to come and collect them?" Poppy glanced at her notice board where she had put her broomstick flying certificate. It might be hidden from the rest of the family by a scrambling-of-letters spell, but she was proud of what she'd achieved.

"There will be a special ceremony on Saturday night."

Amelia shook her head. "I'm not going."

Poppy looked at her in surprise. "Why not?"

Amelia shrugged. *It doesn't feel right,* she messaged.

"Oh dear." The bird flew down from the wardrobe. It ruffled its feathers and changed into a young and pretty witch. "I seem to have this all wrong. I'm Agatha and I'm sorry you don't trust me, though it's always good for a young witch to be cautious. If you're still not sure why don't you ask Mrs Harrison."

"We don't need to. If you know Mrs Harrison it must be all right," Poppy said.

"Then you'll come? I'm so pleased."

"Course we will. Won't we Amelia?"

Amelia frowned.

"We'll see you on Saturday, then." Agatha waved her hand. Her fingers turned into feathers, her arms became wings, and she flew out of the window.

"I'm not going," Amelia said.

"I'm not going on my own."

They glowered at each other until Poppy, who hated falling out with her friend, said, "Why don't we do what Agatha said and ask Mrs Harrison? I'll go on my own if you like."

"It's all right. I'll come with you."

Amelia sounded so reluctant that Poppy nearly told her not to bother, and they still weren't speaking as they walked along the path to the Harrisons' cottage. There was no marmalade cat to greet them and no lights in the workroom.

"They're out." Amelia made for the gate.

"We're not going till I've tried the front door." Poppy ran up the steps and knocked loudly.

It was opened by Mr Harrison, who looked very surprised to see them. "If you've come to see my mother, I'm afraid she's not here."

"When will she be back?"

"She's on holiday in the Caribbean and won't be home until after Christmas. Sorry." Mr Harrison shut the door.

"Great!" Poppy kicked at the path and glowered at Amelia, who couldn't quite hide her smile. Poppy's bad mood lasted all the way home. She didn't even wave goodbye to her friend as Amelia returned to her house.

Poppy stamped into the hall and trampled dirt over the letter that lay on the doormat. Then feeling guilty she picked it up and took it into the kitchen. "It's for you Mum. Sorry," she muttered as she handed it over.

Mum slit open the envelope, took out a piece of paper and stared at it. "Oh!" she said. "Oh!"

"What is it?"

"It's… I don't believe it. I can't even remember entering the competition … but it says here I've won a family holiday for four … to the Caribbean. We must hurry – we're going tomorrow for the whole of Christmas."

The family threw themselves into getting ready. Dad asked Bubbles Mike if he would look after Bernard. Mum found their passports and checked if they had enough sunscreen and everyone started packing. There was so much rushing around that Poppy forgot to tell Amelia what had happened until she saw a message from her saying, *Best news ever. Dad's won a holiday to the Caribbean. Off tomorrow for the whole of Christmas.*

Chapter 23

"HOW WEIRD IS this?" Poppy said when she and Amelia met at the airport.

"We're even going to the same resort," Amelia said. "It's going to be great."

Better than getting a certificate from the Grand Convention of Witches. Poppy quickly blanked the thought. She didn't want to quarrel with her best friend. Not when they were going on the holiday of a lifetime together.

After they passed through to Departures the two girls wandered off to the shops. They were looking at friendship bracelets when Poppy's phone pinged with a message from Mum.

Where are you? We should be boarding. At the same time, Amelia received a text from her dad.

"Don't worry, they won't go without us," Poppy said as they darted through the crowd, but when they reached the gate it had closed and there was no sign of their families.

"What are we going to do?" Amelia gulped back tears.

"Poppy Barrington? Amelia Reeves?" A lady in

uniform approached them. She was carrying a clipboard and wearing dark glasses. "Your families have gone on ahead and I'm going to hurry you through to join them. This way please."

They followed her through a door marked Staff Only, down some stairs and onto the tarmac. The plane was ready for take-off, the fuel tankers were driving away, and the doors were closing.

"Wait for us," Poppy yelled.

"Don't worry. You're already on board. Your glamours are going to have a lovely time." The lady with the clipboard took off her glasses.

"Agatha!" they yelled together, but, before the stunned girls could do anything sensible – like running away – another two witches appeared and bundled them into a white van.

As the vehicle raced up the motorway Poppy rested her elbows on her knees and thought how stupid she'd been. "That holiday was all part of Agatha's plan, wasn't it?"

"I told you not to trust her."

"You were right," Poppy sighed.

"I know." Amelia couldn't help sounding smug. "But we'll get out of here. We've got our broomsticks and I've got an idea."

"If it's what I'm thinking I'm going to need a wee," Poppy said.

"Me too." Amelia winked.

They banged on the sides of the van, drummed their heels on the floor, shouted and yelled and made so much noise that Agatha pulled up at the next service station. She parked the van and opened the doors. Poppy and Amelia jumped out, holding their broomsticks.

"You can't get away like that. Your brooms won't fly."

"Oh no?" Poppy confronted Agatha. "Hover please." The broomstick's twigs rustled. It tried its hardest but it stayed upright.

"It's been disabled," Agatha said smoothly. "For your own good. Hand me your phones then off you go to the toilets and don't be long."

They set off across the parking lot, glancing behind them from time to time to see if Agatha was following. They entered the service station but instead of going to the Ladies they swerved off into the newsagents.

"Excuse me," Poppy said to the girl at the checkout. "Can you help us?"

"Join the queue," the girl said.

"We don't want to buy anything. We need you to call the police. We've been kidnapped. We managed to get out of their van but they're waiting for us outside."

"Now I've heard everything!" The girl raised her eyes to the ceiling.

"It's true. Honestly. They've taken our phones," Amelia said.

"Well…" the girl began.

"I really think you should alert the authorities,"

the woman at the head of the queue intervened. "These girls could be in danger."

"We are," Poppy said.

"Please," Amelia begged.

"Okay. I'll call Security." The girl fumbled in her pocket for her phone.

"It will be all right. They'll be here any minute and until then you are quite safe with us," said the woman at the head of the queue.

At that moment Agatha ran into the shop. "Poppy and Amelia what are you doing? I thought I'd lost you. I've been looking for you everywhere."

"It's her. She's the one that took us," Poppy said. The people in the queue muttered angrily. A large man stepped forward ready to grab Agatha.

The witch smiled and sighed. Looking directly at the girl phoning Security she said, "What have my naughty nieces been saying? Have they told you that they've been kidnapped? Really, you two, you've got to stop doing this." The mutterings from the people in the shop grew louder but this time Poppy and Amelia were the targets of their anger.

"I am so sorry," Agatha turned her smile on the customers. "They get bored on long journeys and start playing these silly games. Last time they were in the power of vampires who were going to suck their blood. Can you imagine?" She spread out her hands and shook her head sadly. "It's so embarrassing. For all of us," she finished softly.

"Emergency over. False alarm." The checkout girl put her phone back in her pocket.

"Come on girls," Agatha said briskly.

"We're not going anywhere with you." Amelia looked around but no one met her glance. The people in the queue stared straight ahead. Other shoppers hurriedly flicked through magazines or showed great interest in the fluffy toys for sale – until a copy of *Mums and Babies* rose from its shelf.

It was followed by *The Daily News.* They fluttered their pages and whirled towards each other, then bowed and floated away. One by one all the newspapers and magazines joined in the dance, followed by the books that flapped their covers in time to the music that blared out across the shop. Lemonade bottles popped their tops and cans exploded sending sprays of sticky sweet bubbles into the air. The bin full of soft toys rocked and swayed spilling its contents over the floor. Toy teddies squeaked, ducks quacked, cats meowed, dogs barked. Sandwiches flew out of the fridge and ice lollies twirled and dripped.

People screamed and stampeded out of the shop. A mother with two small boys in tow barged into Agatha who toppled over the fallen bin and ended up on her back with her legs in the air.

Poppy grabbed Amelia's hand and they ran round the building to the lorry park where a tanker stood with the cab door open, its driver talking to a mate.

"Invisibility spell," Poppy whispered.

"Done," Amelia breathed and they scrambled inside the lorry's cab and crouched down behind the driver's seat.

"Gotta go," the driver said. "The forecast is for heavy snow and I'm on the Newcastle run."

We can't go there. It's miles and miles away, Amelia messaged.

We're not going to, Poppy replied.

"See you mate." The driver slammed the cab door and started the engine.

Poppy screwed up her eyes, concentrated as hard as she could and clicked her fingers. The driver frowned.

"Blow me. I'm on the wrong side of the motorway. How did that happen? Must have been that sat nav. I knew it was on the blink. If I take the next junction I can turn round without losing too much time."

It's a returning-home spell. And it's working! Poppy messaged.

Great, but what do we do when we get home? We're supposed to be in Jamaica, remember.

We'll think of something.

Better had, Amelia replied. *I don't want to spend all Christmas hiding from Agatha and her evil crew.*

Chapter 24

"WHAT ARE YOU doing back here?" the manager of the depot called up to the driver as he parked his lorry in the yard.

"I don't know." The driver scratched his head. "I was on my way to…"

"There's something odd going on." The manager stared into the cab. "You've not given any one a lift, have you? Only I thought I saw…"

The invisibility spell must be wearing off, Poppy messaged.

She and Amelia waited until the two men walked away then jumped down from the lorry and hurried out of the yard.

It was sleeting and splinters of ice stung their hands and faces. "This is really horrid," Amelia said. "We're supposed to be on a nice warm tropical island – not out here in the cold. Let's go home."

"We can't. There's no one there and I don't have a key, but I know where we can go."

"Not to Mrs Harrison's?"

"Course not. She's on holiday. We're going to Mia's."

"To stay with the vampires? I mean Chris and

Hera are all right but..."

"It'll be okay," Poppy said as confidently as she could.

"How are we going to get there?"

"On our broomsticks. They'll take us. Won't you?" Poppy gave her broom a pat and to her relief it wriggled its twigs and bounced up and down. "See, the disabling spell's worn off." She got on her broomstick. Amelia followed suit and they flew into the snow-filled sky. By the time they landed in Mia's garden they were soaked through and so cold that they couldn't stop shivering.

"There are icicles in my hair and my glasses are frosted over," Poppy said.

"I can't feel my feet or my fingers," Amelia said.

"Hurry up and let us in." Poppy banged as hard as she could on the kitchen door until finally it opened.

"What are you doing here?" Mia said.

"They're freezing to death by the look of it," Granny Ghost floated into the room. "Poor dears, they need a bowl of hot soup and a warm towel."

"Got to get the blood circulating or who knows what will happen," Grandpa Ghost said gloomily.

"There's no soup but I'll get some towels," Mia said.

"Put the heating on. I don't know what it is with you vampires but you don't seem to feel the cold," Granny said.

Mia hurried off to do what she'd been told and Granny drifted about tutting her tongue and wringing her hands until Grandpa told her to stop fussing and go and do something useful instead. There wasn't much a ghost could usefully do, but the house was growing warmer and by the time Poppy and Amelia had dried their hair and changed into some of Mia's clothes they were beginning to feel much better.

Chris, Hera and Louis were awake by now and they all gathered in the drawing room to decide what should be done. "Of course you must stay with us until your families come home," Hera said.

"That's great, but what about food?" Mia said.

"No problem. We'll get takeaways for you." Chris was already scrolling down a list of local outlets. "What's your favourite?"

"We like Chinese," Poppy said.

"And pizzas," Amelia added.

"Pizzas it is then."

"What are takeaways, may I ask?" Louis said as Chris sorted out their order.

Mia and her friends exchanged glances. "It's like this all the time. He doesn't know anything about the twenty-first century."

"You can't expect him to, Mia. After all, how much do you know about life in the eighteenth century?" her mother said.

"Or the time of King James, his brother Charles,

the terrible years of the Commonwealth, and the hundreds of years before that?" Louis said.

"Are you that old?" Poppy asked.

"I was made, or rather I became a vampire at the Coronation of Queen Elizabeth, which makes me young for one of our kind."

"Awesome!" Amelia said.

"Absolutely awesome," Poppy added.

"I am a being of great awe." Louis bowed his head graciously in their direction.

"And a pain in the backside," Grandpa Ghost said.

At this point, the front doorbell rang and Poppy and Amelia went to get their food. They ate in the kitchen, watched longingly by Chris and Hera who could still remember the taste of normal food, and with interest by Mia, who had never eaten it. Louis kept asking irritating questions until Granny Ghost told him to be quiet and let the children eat their supper.

There were plenty of unused bedrooms in the vampires' house but Poppy, Amelia and Mia decided to share. "That'll be so nice for Mia. She's never had a sleepover," Granny Ghost said.

"What is a sleepover?" Louis asked.

"It's when your friends come to stay," Mia told him. "You watch films and eat popcorn. I can't do that bit but I've got *The Worst Witch*, *The Addams Family*, *The Book of Life*, *Day of the Dead* and loads more to choose from."

Her bedroom had purple walls, a black ceiling, a huge television, and a large four poster bed. After they'd put on their pyjamas they propped up the pillows and sat and watched *The Monster Squad*. The room was warm, the bed was soft and following their escape from Agatha, Poppy and Amelia were very tired. By the time the film finished, they had both snuggled down under the duvet and were fast asleep.

Mia was too excited to sleep. She'd thought that she'd never be able to do the same things as an ordinary girl and here she was having a sleepover with her best friends. Beside her, Poppy and Amelia breathed softly. Not wanting to wake them she slipped out of bed and crossed over to the window.

She pulled up the blackout blind and looked out at the night. The snow had stopped falling and the sky was bright with stars. The moon was full and silhouetted in front of it was a cat on a broomstick. It was flying straight towards her window. Thinking it was going to crash through the glass Mia jumped back. The broom swerved. The cat leapt off onto the sill, flicked her whiskers with a paw and tapped on the windowpane.

"Ivy?" Mia opened the window. The cat stepped inside, looked around, and seeing Poppy and Amelia jumped onto the bed and began paddling her paws on Poppy's chest.

"Stop it. Get off," Poppy murmured sleepily.

"You've got to wake up. It's urgent. I've been looking for you everywhere." The cat ran her tail under Amelia's nose.

"What's happening?" Amelia sneezed and sat up, rubbing her eyes.

"We need help. Mum and Dad have sealed the cottage. They had to put a protection spell on it. It's like a big bubble that you can't break through unless you're really powerful."

"Why have they done that?"

"Cos of Agatha. She and her fellow witches came looking for Aunt Mortimer. They know her disappearance is something to do with us. Agatha says if we don't tell them where she is by midnight tomorrow they'll pulverise us with their magic."

"Why don't you let them have her?" Poppy said.

"That's what Mum wants. Dad's not so sure. If we give in it will all start again, only worse. Aunt Mortimer will be so angry she'll do anything to destroy us. We've got to stop her, permanently this time."

"Is that why you're here?" Poppy was fully awake.

"If all of us, witches and vampires, work together we can do it," Ivy said.

"We'll do what we can and I'm sure the others from the Flying Broomstick Academy will too, but that won't be enough," Amelia said.

"We don't know enough magic to take on really

powerful witches," Poppy said.

"I know that." Ivy tossed her head impatiently and the cat transformed into a girl. "That's why I'm here. I thought you could ask Mrs Harrison."

"Why don't you?" Mia asked.

"Umm, because she's not very pleased with me," Ivy muttered, her glance skittering around the room as she avoided looking at the other three.

"Why?" Mia sat down beside Poppy, who shuffled over to make room for her.

"Well … it turns out that Mrs Harrison was at school with Aunt Mortimer and even though she knows how evil she is, she thinks what I did was disrespectful. I should never have peed on her." Ivy hung her head then she looked up and her eyes were sparkling. "I don't care if it was a bad thing to do, it was worth it and I'd do it again. But I do care about Mum and Dad and Barbara and Jaspar and Willow and Charlie. They're not strong enough on their own to stand against Agatha and her coven."

"We can't ask Mrs Harrison for help. She's on holiday," Poppy said.

"That's great," Ivy said to their surprise. "Then I won't have to worry about her."

"If she's not there how are we going to find the other witches?" Amelia asked.

"We'll break in and get Mrs H's address book."

"We can't!" Amelia cried.

"We can," Poppy and Mia assured her.

MIA HITCHED A lift on the back of Poppy's broom and they set off for Laburnum Avenue. As before the cottage looked deserted but breaking in to a witch's house wasn't going to be easy.

"It'll be protected by spells against burglars and enemies," Poppy said.

"But not against me," said a small black cat and with a wave of her tail Ivy dived through the cat flap. Minutes later she opened the door and they all crept inside.

"I don't think we should be doing this," Amelia said as they started pulling open the dresser drawers.

"It's an emergency. And it's a good thing we're here because someone's in trouble." Ivy was halfway through changing back into a girl when her tail bristled. She dropped onto four paws and padded over to the cellar door.

"You're right. There's a cat crying down there," Mia said.

"It must be Marmaduke, Mrs Harrison's familiar." Poppy tugged at the handle. "He's got himself locked in. Can you see a key?"

"No, but I might be able to open it." Amelia concentrated very hard. The lock clicked and the door opened far enough for Ivy to slip through.

In the meantime, Mia returned to the search. "Is this what you're looking for?" She held up a slim leather book.

"Let me go," the book squeaked.

"Ouch," Mia yelped. "It bit me."

The lights came on.

"What exactly do you think you are doing?" Mrs Harrison stood in the doorway.

"Rescuing your cat." Ivy came up from the cellar holding Marmaduke in her arms. "He's hungry and thirsty and has been locked in a cage since you went off and left him."

"My poor Marmaduke. Who did this to you? And where's Morfin? I left him in charge while I was away."

"Mother?" Brandishing a rolled-up umbrella Mr Harrison rushed in. "Is it you? I heard voices and I thought we were being burgled."

"No one burgles my house." Mrs Harrison's eyes flashed.

"Except us," Ivy said cheekily.

The witch ignored her. "Why weren't you looking after Marmaduke?" she asked her son.

"Marmaduke?" Mr Harrison looked totally bewildered. "Who's he?"

"Hurrumph!" the witch blew through her nose and crimson, scarlet and vermilion sparks of fury flew about the room. The girls ducked. Mr Harrison shrank back but the witch's anger was directed against someone else. "It's that Agatha.

Not only has she put a forgetting spell on my son but she tricked me into going on a Caribbean holiday. Luckily I was only there for a few days when the magic faded and I realised what had happened."

"It's cos of Agatha we're here." Ivy put Marmaduke down on a chair.

"Agatha?" Mr Harrison blinked.

"Oh go back to bed. I'll explain everything in the morning," his mother said. "A healing spell for Marmaduke first, then you girls can tell me what is going on."

Chapter 25

IT WAS IN the early hours of the morning when the girls returned to Mia's house. "Wherever have you been?" Granny Ghost was waiting for them in their bedroom. "Your parents have been so worried about you, Mia. I did tell them you would be all right but…" She shrugged her ghostly shoulders.

"You better go and tell them what you've been up to." Grandpa Ghost materialised at the foot of the bed.

Hera, Chris and Louis were waiting for them in the drawing room. The lights had been turned down low and the three vampires looked pale and threatening in the gloom. Amelia chewed her lip. Poppy's stomach twisted. And Mia slipped her hands into theirs and squeezed their fingers.

Ivy padded in after them, sat down by the fire, and put her head on one side to show she was listening. She looked so cute and innocent that Poppy felt like strangling her.

"Well," Hera said. "This is not what we expected."

"Sorry," Poppy mumbled and Amelia hung her head.

"We didn't do anything wrong," Mia began. "Well not really…"

The corners of her father's mouth began to twitch.

"It was my fault." Ivy arched her back, stretched and transformed into a girl. "You were the only people I could go to for help." She told them everything that had happened.

When she'd finished Mia said, "We will help Barbara's family, won't we?"

"Just try to stop us." Louis' eyes glowed red. "I haven't had a good fight in—"

"Three hundred years?" Chris was grinning now.

"Far too long. Let me get at those witches." The vampire bared his teeth.

"No you don't. There will be no biting or bloodsucking. Evil witches would make even worse vampires and we don't need any of those," Hera said.

"Mrs Harrison has a plan for us all to work together but before we tell you what she said, is there any of that pizza left?" Ivy asked hopefully.

Poppy and Amelia shook their heads.

"No problem. I'll order some more. Twenty-four-hour express delivery." Chris took out his phone.

They only had to wait a few minutes before the doorbell rang.

"That's the second time tonight I've been to this

address. Are you having a party?" the delivery man asked.

Poppy shook her head. "We got hungry again."

"Very hungry. All this talk of food..." Louis loomed up behind her.

"Eeek!" The delivery man jumped back on his motorbike and sped away.

"You shouldn't have done that." Poppy turned around, but Louis was nowhere to be seen.

WHILE EVERYONE ELSE sat and discussed Mrs Harrison's plan for dealing with Agatha and her evil witches, Louis decided that he would tackle them on his own.

Flying to the witches' meeting place he hovered above them while Agatha outlined her tactics for the attack on Willow Cottage. When she finished she raised her arms and cried, "Together we are one. Together we will prevail. Together we will win."

"We will win!" roared the rest of the coven.

"Never!" With a swirl of his cloak, Louis landed in the middle of their circle. "Avaunt ye witches! Take yourselves and your evil from this place! Depart and never trouble this city again."

"Who are you that dares interrupt our

ceremonies?" Agatha advanced on the vampire.

"I am Louis de Courcey, a vampire of great power, and I command you to be gone."

"Pshaw!" Agatha gave him a withering look. "If you think you can tell me what to do then you are truly mistaken." She raised her hand and pointed. Louis, afraid that he was going to be turned into something unpleasant, hurriedly transformed into a bat. Agatha clicked her fingers. Louis fluttered his wings but however hard he tried he could not break free of the enchantment that bound him.

"You are rubbish!" Agatha said and the other witches broke into gales of laughter as the bat's wings stiffened and hardened. His body lost all feeling, his eyes dimmed, and he fell to the ground. Agatha picked up the plastic bat and dropped it in the nearest litter bin.

Chapter 26

POPPY, AMELIA, MIA and Ivy slept together, curled up in Mia's four poster bed through the whole of the next day. Hera woke them late in the evening and while the three young witches ate their Chinese take-a-way they went over the gathering spell Mrs Harrison had taught them.

"I hope I remember it all. It's really, really important to get it right," Amelia fretted.

"You will. We all will." Poppy crossed her fingers.

She tried to look confident and so did the others, but even Ivy was nervous when the time came to leave for the gathering.

They said goodbye to the ghosts and vampires, mounted their broomsticks and headed towards Laburnum Avenue. Below them the streetlights were veiled in a fine curtain of snow which blurred the outlines of streets and houses, making it difficult to see where they were going. Leaning low on her broom Poppy peered through the dimness until she spotted a patch of vivid colour.

"We're here," she called over her shoulder and the three girls landed in the Harrison's garden, where a fire of blue and emerald flames was burning brightly.

The door of the cottage opened and Mrs Harrison in her witch's robes, with Marmaduke at her heels, came out to greet them.

"Now we are all here we can begin. You know what you have to do?"

"Yes I do," Poppy croaked, swallowing the awkward lump that seemed to have settled in her throat.

"Yes." Amelia's voice was higher than usual.

Ivy, unable to think of anything clever or outrageous to say, nodded.

"Take your places and we will begin."

One in each corner, they made a square around the fire. Mrs Harrison raised her arms and began, "From the lands of the North and all regions before and beyond, I summon you."

"From the lands of the East and all regions before and beyond, I summon you," Poppy said.

"From the lands of the South and all regions before and beyond, I summon you," Amelia said.

"From the lands of the West and all regions before and beyond, I summon you." Ivy was the last to speak.

"Come to our aid, help us in our time of need," they finished together.

As the last word left their lips there was a whoosh and a small fat wizard, with a large tabby cat perched on his broom, landed beside them. He was followed by Primrose, her parents and their familiars; then came Su Lin and her mum with their blue eyed Siamese, Vivica and her parents on brooms balanced with huge Norwegian Forest Cats, an elderly wizard with a pointed hat and round spectacles on the end of his nose, and a pair of beautiful witches with long green hair and— On and on they came until the garden was full of warlocks, wizards, witches and their familiars.

"We fight to save our sisters and brothers from Agatha and her coven," Mrs Harrison told the gathering. "It will not be easy. We will have to use all our combined powers but we are wise and strong, and good will always triumph over evil."

The witches, wizards and warlocks cheered. The cats meowled their support. Everyone mounted their broomsticks.

I'm a bit scared, Poppy confessed as she and Amelia flew side by side.

Me too but we have to help Barbara.

Witches together. Primrose whizzed past. "No problem," she called over her shoulder.

"Brilliant fun." Vivica waved a hand in the air.

Showing off again, Poppy thought.

Or pretending not to be scared, Amelia messaged. *We'll be all right. We've just got to remember what to do.*

Poppy's grip on her broomstick tightened as they raced towards Broome Compton. After they arrived Mrs Harrison and her witches circled the magic shield that surrounded Willow Cottage like a great plastic bubble, chanting protection spells and sealing any weak points while keeping a look out for Agatha and her coven.

For a while nothing happened, then with a rush of air, a V-shaped formation swept out of the darkness towards them.

"Avenge Mortimer." Agatha raised her wand and bolts of magic zigzagged through the air.

"They've made a hole in the shield," one of the green-haired witches screamed. "Help me close it."

Witches and warlocks flew to her aid, sweeping Poppy along with them. Pointing their wands they wove a web of words and the gash began to close.

Urged on by Agatha, her coven redoubled their efforts. The bubble splintered and cracked. Mrs Harrison's witches did their best to mend it, but they were being beaten back. Wands blazed and sparked.

A sizzle of light struck Amelia and her broomstick nosedived. A flash from Agatha's wand and Poppy screamed as she was hit in the chest. Her hands went numb and she hurtled towards Amelia, who grabbed at her as they fell through a hole in the shield and crash landed headfirst into a snow drift.

Spitting out a mouthful of snow, Poppy heaved herself onto her hands and knees. Beside her, Amelia rolled over onto her back and was staring at the sky. There was a dark patch where the protection spell had shattered.

"The hole is getting bigger," Amelia said in a small voice.

"Look out!" Primrose tumbled towards them, falling hard on her bottom.

Another crack appeared in the bubble and Ivy's broom corkscrewed downwards. At the last moment it straightened up and Ivy glided to a halt. "It's bad. The shield is failing. We're going to have to make a run for it. I'm going to tell Mum and Dad to get everyone out of the house." Picking up her broom she raced towards the cottage just as a bat whizzed past her ear.

"The vampires are here!" Poppy yelled.

There were shrieks and groans and bangs and crackles. Flashes and jagged shards of magic ripped through the bubble. The snow-covered garden lit up like a funfair. Familiars howled and hissed, snarled and spat.

The last of the shield fell away and Agatha and Mrs Harrison landed their brooms. Face to face, they confronted each other.

"How dare you," Agatha hissed pointing her finger. "This is my fight."

"I will not stand for your evil." Mrs Harrison raised her hand.

"Enough!" Mia's father, his cloak swirling behind him, fangs gleaming, eyes blood red, stepped between them.

"You can't tell us what to do." Both witches turned on the vampire. Chris smiled a blood chilling smile.

"Oh no?" He looked so terrifying that even the witches backed away. "Neither side is winning this battle. We can let you continue until you destroy each other, or we can broker a peace deal. The choice is yours."

"And if we don't agree?" Agatha said.

"Then neither of you will leave this garden alive." Hera landed beside her husband.

"We want Mortimer back," Agatha said.

"And we want you to leave the family at Willow Cottage alone," Mrs Harrison said.

"I agree. Let the spell be lifted and our sister returned to us." Agatha looked at Barbara's parents.

Ambrose and Belinda joined hands with their daughters and murmured a reversing spell. The drive heaved, snow fountained upwards, gravel shot in all directions, and a figure rose from the ground. Hair writhing like snakes, face smeared with dirt, Miss Mortimer advanced on her sister.

"How could you do this to me?" she snarled. "As for you..." She glared malevolently at Ivy. "What you did was disgusting beyond words and you should be—"

"Leave it, Mortimer," Agatha drawled. "It's over. No more harassing your family. We're leaving." Broomstick in hand she surveyed the pupils of the Flying Broomstick Academy. "If any of you girls want to join us, now is the time." She switched on a smile and the cruel evil Agatha became a pretty young woman with a kind face. "If you want every one of your wishes to be granted and anyone who has ever hurt or annoyed you to be punished for what they did, then come with me. I can promise you a life of excitement and fun. No hard work required—" Mrs Harrison pulled a face "—just everything you've always wanted."

The apprentice witches looked at each other.

"She can't mean that?" Su Lin said. "Nothing in life comes without hard work."

"Doesn't sound right to me, but…" Primrose looked at her mum who was shaking her head and muttering about the dark path.

"I'm not going anywhere," Barbara said.

"Nor me," Poppy and Amelia spoke together and moved closer to Mrs Harrison who gave them an encouraging nod.

"Well done girls," she said quietly.

"What about you?" Agatha pointed to Vivica. "You look like a girl who knows what's good for her."

Don't go with her. Poppy might not like Vivica very much but she didn't want her going over to Agatha and her evil ways.

"Sorry. Not my sort of thing at all."

"That's our girl." Vivica's dad put his hand on

her shoulder.

"Fine. Let's go," Agatha said.

"Not yet. My niece hasn't chosen."

"Who me? I'm not choosing anything or anyone," Ivy meowed as she turned into a cat. Her dad swallowed and put one arm around his wife, the other around Barbara, while Ivy purred and twined herself around their legs.

"Well if that's the way you want it. You don't know what you're missing." Agatha stuck her nose in the air, mounted her broomstick, and she and her witches flew away.

"We did it," Mia said after the last of them had gone.

"You did indeed." Barbara's dad gave his family a big hug. "Let's celebrate our victory."

"Come in and we'll party till dawn." Belinda held open the door. "Everyone is welcome."

"Thank you." Chris took Hera's hand and the witches, wizards and warlocks followed the vampires into the house.

Poppy, Amelia and Mia were the last to leave the garden.

"That was the most amazing night ever," Amelia said.

"It was awesome," Poppy agreed. "Specially when Mia's mum and dad arrived."

"It was scary but good and now we're going to a party." Mia's face shone, then she frowned. "Only thing is, has anyone seen Louis?"

Chapter 27

LOUIS WAS IN a rubbish bin. He was sticky with coke and greasy from the crisp packet that lay on top of him. There was a gob of chewing gum on his wing and he was lying on a half-eaten cheese and pickle sandwich.

Being plastic he couldn't move but his insides twisted and churned. Was this how he was going to end? Not in a duel with a vampire hunter, or a fight with a powerful witch, but lost and forgotten on a rubbish heap?

Meanwhile, Poppy, Amelia and Mia were sitting cross-legged on Mia's four poster bed. The curtains were drawn and they were talking about the battle of the night before.

"Something must have happened to Louis. He was really looking forward to fighting Agatha and her coven," Poppy said.

"We should go and look for him but where do we start?" Amelia said.

"The Downs," Mia said. "I think that's where he would have gone."

"To deal with the witches on his own? Sounds like Louis," Poppy agreed.

Amelia pulled back a curtain. "It's grey and

horrible out there so no one will see us if we go on our broomsticks."

"Can I ride with you Poppy?" Mia was tired after the battle. It took a lot of energy to transform from girl to bat and back again.

The two girls sat on Poppy's broom and side by side with Amelia they flew out of the window.

The Downs stretched for miles but Poppy had a good idea about where Agatha's coven might meet. They hovered over the elder grove scanning every shadow for a possible clue but there was no sign of Louis.

"We must have got it wrong," Poppy said.

"No." Mia wrinkled her nose. She sniffed, then sniffed again. "Louis has been here. I can smell him. Fly over there Poppy, towards that rubbish bin. Yes, the scent's getting stronger."

"It's the bin. They always pong," Amelia said.

"Not of old vampires they don't," Mia retorted. "Hurry up, Poppy. The bin lorry's here."

The broom accelerated, but it was too late. By the time they reached the bin the rubbish was being tipped into the back of the lorry.

"Oh no!" Mia groaned.

"It's all okay. You must have got it wrong. Louis wasn't there or we'd have seen him," Poppy said.

"We would if he'd been in human form but what if he was a bat?"

"Or Agatha changed him into something

nasty," Amelia said.

"I'm going to summon her." Poppy landed and held out her hands. "It will work better if you help me."

"You can't," Amelia said fearfully.

"I can." After the battle with Agatha and her coven Poppy was feeling fearless. "Mia, we need you too."

"I'm not a witch."

"It doesn't matter. You're one of us and we can't leave Poppy to do this on her own." Amelia took Mia's hand.

The three girls formed a circle and Poppy chanted a summoning spell. Within seconds a very angry Agatha zoomed in, riding her broom like a rocket.

"Yes?" she hissed.

"What did you do to Louis?" Poppy said.

"Oh, you mean that pathetic attempt at a vampire. He was such rubbish that I disposed of him."

"In that bin?" Amelia pointed.

Agatha shrugged. "What does it matter which bin. I got rid of him."

"We want him back. We made a pact. You got Miss Mortimer, we want Louis."

"Too late. Poor little plastic bat has had it."

"No he hasn't." Mia's eyes blazed with anger. "Either you release him from the spell or I call Chris and Hera and tell them you broke the agreement."

"Oh well, if you're going to be difficult about it I'll wander off to the depot and see what can be done."

"We're coming with you." Poppy didn't trust Agatha. She was sure that given the opportunity the witch would leave it too late to save Louis.

"If you insist, but the chances are the compactor is already crunching the rubbish into tiny pieces."

"Then we'd better hurry."

The three witches and Mia flew across the city towards the recycling plant.

"How do we know which one Louis is in?" Poppy asked as one by one the Council lorries drove up to empty their loads.

"I memorised the registration. Look, there it is." Mia pointed.

Poppy flew as low as she dared. The lorry moved into position at the conveyor belt. The hopper tipped up and rubbish spilled out. Most of it was squashed beyond recognition but Mia leaned from the broom and peered intently at the mess.

"There. That tiny bat. That's Louis."

"Agatha." Poppy turned her broomstick so that she was facing the witch. "Change him back."

Agatha heaved a great sigh.

"Do it." Mia bared her fangs.

"Very well. If that's what you want."

Poppy nudged her broomstick closer. Mia's

eyes turned red.

Agatha clicked her fingers and Louis' body appeared on top of the rubbish.

"Stop the belt," one of the bin men yelled. People came running from all sides and the machinery ground to a halt.

"Happy now?" Agatha waved her hand and disappeared into a cloud of dark magic. No one tried to stop her – they were too worried about what was happening to Louis.

"He's not breathing," Poppy said.

"Old vampires don't," Mia said.

"So why doesn't he get up?"

"I don't know. Perhaps he's hurt."

"We've got to help him but there's too many people about."

"The police are coming. I can hear the sirens."

"Tell him to turn into a bat, Mia." Amelia bent low on her broomstick. "Whew!" she yelled, dive bombing the supervisor. "Look at me!" She whizzed over the workers' heads flying so close that some of them had to duck. "See. No hands." Gripping her broom with her knees she spread her arms. "I'm like a bat," she shrieked, hoping Louis received the message and to her relief the battered body of a vampire melted away into a small furry animal.

Got him, Poppy messaged as she grabbed the creature. "Mia, get the forgetting powder out of my pocket and chuck it over everyone."

"Done," Mia said.

Home, Poppy messaged. Amelia waved and turned back towards the vampires' house.

"THAT WAS CLOSE." Poppy landed in Mia's bedroom.

"I don't want to do that ever again." Amelia came to a halt beside her.

"You don't? Consider how I feel. I am covered in grease and slime and I reek." Back in human shape Louis held his nose. "I must go and take a bath forthwith and immediately."

"You could say thank you. After all we saved your life," Poppy called as the vampire rushed out of the room.

"Not Louis. He doesn't do that sort of thing," Mia said.

"Well he should."

"He's been very badly brought up." Amelia giggled.

"He's a disgrace to the vampire race," Mia cried and they all burst out laughing.

CHRISTMAS MORNING WITH the vampires was the strangest Poppy and Amelia had ever known. There were stockings full of presents on the end of the four-poster bed, and when these had been opened they flew to Willow Cottage for Christmas dinner. Barbara's parents had cooked turkey with all the trimmings and Mia had a bowl of cheese and onion crisps all to herself. In the evening, back at Mia's, there were games in the drawing room with the vampires and Granny and Grandpa Ghost. Then the girls went to bed and the vampires partied.

The day before school started Poppy and Amelia returned home. When Poppy walked into the kitchen it was as if she'd never been away. Dad was making tea and Mum was reading her messages. "Is your uniform ready for tomorrow?" she asked.

Before Poppy could answer, Jake ran in with Bernard yapping at his heels.

"Will you play with me Poppy?" he said.

"It would be really helpful." Mum looked up from her screen. "There's so much to do before we go back to work. I don't know where the time's gone. I can't even remember what we did over Christmas. Can you?"

She looked at Dad, who shook his head, and said, "What about you Poppy? Did you enjoy Christmas?"

Poppy thought about being kidnapped by the

evil Agatha, battling with the witches, rescuing Louis from the tip, and spending Christmas Day with the vampires.

"It was awesome," she said. "Absolutely awesome."

Also by Misha Herwin

The Adventures of Letty Parker

Set in an alternative Victorian Bristol, the Letty Parker adventures see our girl-detective and her friends battle the Dark Ones, dragons, pirates, witches, solving mysteries, and rescuing missing people and finding magical gems in a series of fabulous adventures.

City of Secrets

Bridge of Lies

Island of Fear

Published by The Penkhull Press